YOU BUT NOT YOU

Hollie Hughes

ISBN-13: 9798425271686

For You

ONE

I rest my palm on the steel plate of the door, and wait for the cool to permeate my skin, to momentarily still my thoughts. It can only be a few seconds, a miniscule fraction of a life, and yet it is an instant I feel I could disappear into forever. I don't want to startle him, but he jumps anyway, and we both laugh. The atmosphere in the room has changed; there's a different kind of energy in here now. I hope that means it's worked.

'Everything ok?' I ask.

'Yes, fine, it was easier than I thought actually – a bit like meditation, but without the pressure.'

I smile. He is not the sort of person you can imagine meditating, much less feel any pressure over it. I move to turn off the camera, and he stands to join me at the table. He picks up a lens, inspects it, puts it down again, smiles, then absentmindedly circles the lens in a figure of eight on the table, like a magician about to perform a trick, smiles again. I resist the urge to tell him to stop, even though I know I will not be able to keep myself from turning the lens over and over again in my own hands later. I have never liked anyone touching my work

1

stuff. He seems to sense my discomfort. It must be my turn to speak.

'Emily should be back in a minute,' I say. 'She'll see you out. I'm not sure where she's got to. I would've waited but I thought you might be getting restless.'

'It's fine,' he says. 'I'm not in any rush.'

I think how irritating it must be for him to still be here, and how he must be silently scanning through all the other places he needs to be today, his mind already running on to the next commitment. I wonder how many years of practise it has taken for him to perfect that seemingly effortless air of amiable politeness when inside he must be screaming at the mundanity of it, of being here now – with me.

'Actually, I thought I might have a look round after.'

He does that 'caught-out' smile he used to do in his early films then, and it occurs to me that I was right about that all along. It was something he'd brought into his craft from life, to begin with, but was able to let go of once it was no longer needed, like a child ditching stabilisers. It's strangely affecting that he's held onto it in the real world though, and I feel myself flush at the realisation. I don't know why. I do know why. I don't want to look at him. And I really don't want to make eye contact, even though I have often wondered what the exact colour of his eyes will be. I keep mine fixed firmly on the lenses. In just a few seconds, Emily will be back. I think of the extraordinary lengths I have taken to bring all this about. I know I won't get this opportunity again. I need to say something, anything.

'Look, this is weird, I know, and you must get this all the time. I just wanted to tell you – I didn't ask you to do this because it's you. I mean, it was because it's you, but not for the reasons you most likely think. I watched all your films. Not after I'd already asked you to do this – before. Anyway, I watched all your films, and I got the idea to do this because of you. It wasn't because it was you, it was because of you.'

Careful, you're going to go too far with this. I try to lighten my tone, but it doesn't quite work.

'Basically, I just think you're brilliant. I mean, your work is brilliant' I say. 'Like, seriously underrated.'

Underrated? I almost can't believe I have said it. It's not like it's not true, but then what am I saying by saying it? I'm still focusing on the lenses, and he crouches down so that he can look up at me to make eye contact. He is close enough that I am reluctant to breathe.

'All my films?' he says. 'Even the ones where I...'

'Yes, even those' I say.

I can feel myself flushing again, beads of perspiration forming under my makeup, ready to break out and make this even more painful than it already is. The sound of the door opening makes us both jump, and we laugh again.

'So sorry,' Emily says. 'I got caught up in something. How did it go? Everything ok?'

'All good,' he says and, seemingly incapable of speech, I smile and nod inanely.

'Right then, I'll see you out, although you're more than welcome to stay and look around, of course. We have some wonderful temporary exhibitions on at the moment. I can arrange a guide for you, if you'd like?'

She turns to me. 'Kate, shall I leave you to finish up here?'

'Yes, that's fine,' I manage. 'I'll be another ten minutes or so.'

She nods. 'I'll come back for you after I've seen James out.'

'Kate,' he says. 'It's been really lovely to meet you. I'll keep an eye out for what you do next. And thanks again for asking me.'

He takes my hand, as if to shake it, but then just closes his other hand around it. A jolt of static runs through me, and I have never been so conscious of my raggedy bitten fingernails in my life.

'Thank you so much,' I say. 'We'll let you know when it opens.'

'Yes, of course,' says Emily. 'We'll have all the arrangements sent over to Julie.'

She is smiling, holding the door open for him now, politely waiting for him to cross the room, and then they are gone. I don't look up from the lenses to see if he looks back at all. Why would he?

Afterwards, I sit on a bench outside, watching the river go by, drinking coffee. I've probably sat in this exact same spot before, maybe when Max and Josh were young, or maybe even before that, when it was just me and Dan. I don't remember exactly though. I don't want to go home. All the possibility has gone from the day, but I am not yet ready for it to end. The feeling of hyperreality is still to dissipate, and this has not been the defining moment I thought it would. I thought, after today, I would know where things were going – whether this would change things for me, or whether I would just get back on the train and go back to normal. Or my kind of normal anyway. I thought I would feel different somehow, more certain one way or the other.

The same school group from earlier emerge from the gallery and settle down with their packed lunches on the grass, chattering excitedly as they unwrap tinfoil packages and spike plastic straws into drinks cartons. There won't be too many more days left like this, when it will still be warm enough to sit out for lunch, this year. One of the girls catches my eye and I cast her a smile. Shyly, she returns it. They're infants still – Year 1 or 2. About the same age Max must have been when James had his first big film come out, I think. He'd been in a few things before that, of course, but I didn't know that at the time. I feel an involuntary bubbling of something almost like laughter rising up in my chest, and I can't quite help the smile that my lips somehow form themselves into. One meeting in an art gallery, and he has become 'James' to me – not James Talisker, the actor, but James, as in just James, as if I somehow know him now that we're on first name terms. As if he will ever think of me again after today.

The girl thinks I am smiling at her again, and waves. I wave back. I can remember one of the mums going on about the film at the time – she'd already been to see it twice.

'Why don't you come too?' she'd said. 'I don't mind going again.'

It had seemed almost outrageously decadent to me, the thought that I might go and watch a film in the daytime whilst Max was at school – and I still had Josh at home anyway. I'd laughed about it then, at the mum with her slightly over the top interest in some teen movie and the teen actor.

It didn't seem seedy or anything, just amusing. I have forgotten her name now, although I can still picture her clearly, and I can remember that she was French. It bothers me that her name is lost to me though, she was one of the few mums I'd liked. She'd moved away not long after and we weren't friendly enough to keep in touch. I'd watched the films since, when they were on TV, and then I'd read the books too. They made me feel young again I suppose. That's what I hadn't really under-stood about the mum at the time – it was her own youth she'd been longing for, not theirs.

I need to be able to remember today because, if nothing else does change after this, this day will have to be enough. This one day where I took the most ordinary of lives and turned it into some-thing extraordinary, even if only for a moment. I need to run it through in my mind to make sure it gets filed properly, uncorrupted. So, I do not think of how the day will end – of the train journey, the taxi ride from the station, the familiar smell of home, the evening meal, Me and Dan slumped in front of the TV, the boys in their rooms. I think instead of how it started, and of each seg-ment thereafter. The equipment already stowed in the hallway the evening before. The outfit so carefully selected as to appear completely random, clothes hung in the wardrobe ready and waiting days earlier, the makeup so painstakingly applied, the inevitable scramble for the train when, in the end, I didn't leave nearly enough time to get ready as I ought to have done. The thinking time on the train, which went all too quickly. How I oh so carefully, and pointlessly as it turned out, planned out what I would say to him. Lines written and rehearsed for a performance that never happened, and now never would. My arrival at the gallery, the introduction to the girl – Emily. How the two of us had sat side by side in reception. Me visibly nervous, her probably just as bad, I'd thought, but better at hiding it. The school children rushing in excitedly through the revolving doors, and the few stray auburn leaves they pulled in with them. How the guide welcomed the group, ushering them on to their first experience or workshop, and how the leaves were left behind, fluttering slightly, as if they might change tack and take off again with each new person that came in. How I'd wondered if the leaves would be gone by the time we were finished. How I'd missed him coming in, but how Emily had not. How she'd rushed over to greet him, and I'd been left scrabbling with all the equipment. If only I'd got there earlier. If I'd managed to be at all professional about it, I could have already been set up in the room and waiting.

Emily had made the introductions, even though she'd only just met him herself. I'd marvelled at how easily she seemed to manage it all, manage this whole strange thing, managed me, him. But then I suppose she was younger than him, and much younger than me, and maybe this sort of thing happened all the time in her world. Maybe it would in mine too, if everything changed for me after this in the way that Karl had said it would. I'd tried so hard not to notice the stares, as we'd made the awkward walk through the hall, up to the mezzanine floor, and then along the corridor to the installation room.

And then the segment where I'd had to set everything up, kicking myself again that I hadn't done all this beforehand. It must have seemed like such an imposition to him, that he'd had to wait while I'd got everything ready, but he hid it well enough. I thanked god for Emily, as she continued to chat to him about his journey, the weather, what he was working on now and next, how this was going to be the pivotal moment of the season, of, let's face it, the year. Everything was ready, and I was ready, and all that was left for me to do was to position him and position the camera. I'd told him to sit level centre in the chair, facing the camera head on.

'Can I move at all?' he'd asked.

'Yes, you can move,' I'd said. 'But try not to move your body too much, if you can. It's fine to move your head, but only as you. It's really important you don't act.'

He'd nodded then. It seemed like he'd understood but I'd had to be sure. I had to get it right. 'You have to commit to just sitting there for a couple of hours' I'd said.

Of course, I was sounding like a complete dick, but I couldn't stop myself.

'You have to just think to yourself 'Ok, I'm going to just sit here for a couple of hours, and I'm going to just think of whatever comes into my mind, or nothing, if nothing comes into my mind, and it's fine if nothing does. But, if something does come into my mind, then that's fine too. I'm going to mostly look at the camera, unless I forget and look away, which is also fine, but I'm not going to act. Whatever happens, I'm not going to act."

'A couple of hours?' he'd asked.

'Yes, a couple of hours. Sorry – is that going to be a problem?'

He'd had me panicked then. I'd supposed if he could only do twenty minutes or an hour it would have to do. What could I say? But it wouldn't be what I'd sold to the gallery.

'No, that's fine, a couple of hours. I get it.'

And I realised then that he did get it. He'd seemed so relaxed, so compliant, as if he was used to this sort of thing happening all the time. But, then again, he is an actor after all, and clearly used to taking direction, and maybe this sort of thing does happen all the time in filming anyway. But still, he seemed to be placing a lot more confidence in me than I felt in myself.

'So, it's all running,' I'd said. 'Obviously I'll cut all this stuff out later.'

'Obviously.'

Such an idiot – of course he was used to this. He'd smiled at me then, not at me and Emily, but me – just me. He feels sorry for me, I'd thought, he's embarrassed for me – he's trying to be encouraging.

'Right, so it's all running. I'll be just along the corridor. If you do need to come out for anything, just come out. I'll make sure no one comes in. All you have to do is sit there and wait – but don't wait, just sit there.'

'Ok, wait, but don't wait. I think I can manage it.'

Emily had stifled a giggle. 'We'll leave you to it then' she'd said, taking charge again, gently ushering me out and, even as I'd bristled at the intervention, I was nevertheless grateful for it.

The two hours had passed quickly – almost too quickly. Emily had picked me up a coffee before disappearing back to wherever she was based, and I was left alone to my thoughts. I'd brought a book with me, but ended up reading the same page three times before giving up completely and scrolling my social media accounts instead. I could've posted something about today, but there was still a part of me that thought it might not happen, that he'd change his mind, and it would have felt a bit cheap to do that anyway. I didn't want him to regret it afterwards. It was a strange thing for him to have agreed to in the first place – although maybe not quite so strange if you knew as much about him as I did. It wasn't just the films, there was all the interview footage I'd watched too. I don't dare add up the hours.

It had started at the end of Summer. I'd taken the boys to the cinema for the latest action thing. There was a bit more to it than that, but I was finding it hard to concentrate. I didn't realise it was him at first – he wasn't the main character, so he didn't get much screen time to begin with – but, eventually, it hit me, that it was James Talisker, all grown up. On the way home, I'd said that I hadn't known it was a James Talisker film, and how much he'd changed since those films he'd been in all those years ago. I felt self-conscious saying his name out loud even then, even on that day, even before all this had started.

'Oh, yeah, those' Max had replied. 'James Talisker was the only decent thing to come out of that franchise. He's actually quite a good actor – he's done loads of indie stuff since then.'

So, I re-watched the teen franchise. Watching them again made me feel strangely very old, and yet inexplicably young, both at the same time. Somehow it seemed ok to like him in those films now that he was all grown up, in a way that it wouldn't have felt quite right to at the time. By now, I'd looked up his entire filmography, so I knew that he was actually early twenties when those first few films were made anyway. Like that made it ok.

I started working my way through his back list – most of them weren't films I would usually watch, but I'd already passed that particular point of return some way back. I'd never done this with an actor before – it was like when you read a book you love and then binge read every other book the author ever wrote. I kept expecting to get satiated, and then bored, but the reverse was true – the more I watched, the more I wanted to watch. The more I saw, the more I wanted to see.

Then there was the interview footage – I found it fascinating how he had cannibalised so much of himself to begin with but then, in the more recent films, it was like he was starting again from scratch each time. Although perhaps all actors did this, and I just wasn't paying enough attention before. The way he spoke about his work was exhilarating too – he was shy to show how seriously he took it, and how exciting he found it, but he spoke about it anyway. It's the way I am when talking about my work. And that was the problem really – I was starting to see too many connections between us that simply weren't there, because there were none.

It started to feel a bit out of control – I knew it wasn't quite right, but I didn't really know how to stop. I wasn't entirely sure I could even, and I began to wonder how far I would go with it. Most people would admit to a celebrity crush, but when does it become more than that, more than just a bit of fun, something a bit more serious, something altogether more sinister? Looking back now, it was probably when it got to the point where I would be embarrassed if anyone found out. It wasn't like I would have ever stood outside a film set screaming, or stalked his hotel, or anything like that. But then, maybe, what I'd done in the end was actually worse than all of that, far worse – because I had somehow managed to engineer a situation where I could legitimately meet him.

And then there was the art, and I wasn't altogether sure where the obsession ended, and the art began. And isn't all art obsession anyway? Once I'd got the idea for the project, there was no going back. It had become a compulsion. Even as I had felt physically sick writing to his agent that first time, it had become something I had to do over something I might do, over something I might like to do. I've tried to work out if I'd have got the idea for the project independently of him, if I hadn't completely saturated myself in him beforehand that is. But, even if I had, he would still have been the most obvious choice of subject anyway. My face burns each time I turn the word 'subject' over in my mind because, as much as I might have tried to convince myself a thousand times that it's not just about the way he looks, there is no getting away from the inescapable truth that he is quite simply the most astonishingly beautiful person I have ever seen, or am ever likely to see, in my life. And, even if I had seen more in him since, it was the way he looked that made me want to see more in the first place. And now that I had seen him in real life, talking, moving, being, in real life, I hated myself even more for it. I'd felt even more ashamed than ever. It felt like a betrayal. And it was a betrayal of self too. Sitting there in that corridor, waiting to go back in and take the camera down, I'd felt less in control of myself than I had ever done in my life before. It was as if all the feelings I'd experienced, watching the films and the footage, were simply a diluted form of everything I was feeling now. I knew I was going to have to go back in that room again, and look at him, and talk to him, just like

I'd had to do earlier. Only this time I didn't have to wonder about how it would feel, I knew exactly how it would feel – and it terrified me. It was a level of intoxication, above anything, treacherous.

This has to be enough now, I think. The temperature has dropped, and so too has the light. There is no warmth in the air at this time of year, only in the sun. I stand up from the bench, and roll back my shoulders. As I pick up my cases, and turn in the direction of the tube, I can't help but glance up at the gallery behind me though, one last time – just as the late afternoon light breaks through the clouds for a moment, and catches on the tiniest glint of auburn in one of the upper gallery windows. A face that is only just visible as it turns away. And then I walk away too, back to normality, carrying that tiny little glint of auburn extraordinary with me as I go.

TWO

Dan barely even looks up from his tablet as I walk in which, tonight, is more of a relief than an irritation. I call up to the boys, but don't get much response, so head straight out to the kitchen. I'm not even sure I've penetrated the headphones.

'You're late.'

He's followed me out.

'The trains were bad.'

'How was college?'

'Good. Actually, I've got to go in quite a bit over the next few weeks, just while we're finishing off.'

'What about work?'

'It's ok, I've got loads of weddings on at the moment, so not much going on during the week anyway.'

'So we won't be seeing much of you then?'

'No.'

He wanders back into the lounge, and I start opening cupboards and piling up the components of a meal on the worktop. I choose pasta so I can do it on auto-pilot. I still can't quite believe I've not told him, but I can hardly tell him now. It will seem odd – as if I've deliberately tried to withhold it somehow. I wonder how long it will be before he finds out. A few weeks of getting everything ready, and then the opening. I won't take him, and he wouldn't want to go anyway, so I suppose it depends on if it gets in the papers or not. Hopefully, it will reach the art mags, but it's unlikely to break through beyond that – unless James comes to the launch or anything, which also seems unlikely. Even then, it's only going to be in the celebrity pages, and Dan doesn't read anything like that. So it will probably be when someone else mentions it to him. I can't quite work out yet how he's going to react, and I realise I don't care that much either. I care more about the fact that I don't care.

I should do something about it, about me and Dan, but none of the options appeal, so I shelve it in a box marked 'pending'. And why should I have to be the one to instigate something anyway? What is it about women that we make ourselves responsible for both the making of a marriage, and for the dismantling of it? It can wait until after the opening and graduation, at least. This is not how I imagined a marriage would end – not in storms and tears, as I have always supposed, but in empty silence, and resignation. Although perhaps, after all, this is how all marriages do end, and it just takes some longer than others to get here.

After dinner, I play Scrabble with the boys. Josh wins for a change, which is nice. Max usually wins at everything, and that's got to sting a bit. I know I should be grateful that they still want to spend time with me at their age, and I am. They'll be away at uni soon enough, and then it will just be me and Dan, stretching further and further away from one another into the distance. I don't know what is worse – the panic I am feeling now, or the feeling that the panic will soon be over, and then it will be too late. Not too late for a change, I don't believe that, just too late for anything meaningful.

Back when we were kids, adults used to joke about this person or that person having a mid-life crisis – it was always the person doing the crazy thing that was the subject of the joke, and everyone else, the ones who were able to recognise and resist the pull of the mid-life crisis themselves, the sensible, normal ones. But now I am here, I see the panic for what it is, for what it was. There were those that acted on it, and then there were those that squashed it down and repressed it, but they all felt it. Just as I am feeling it, and just as Dan surely must be. But it seems to me that this repression is the cruellest of drugs - a protection in the moment, a death in the end. And, like the worst kind of addicts, we are all co-dependent.

Sometimes I wish I hated him – it would be easier that way. It would be so much easier to do something, anything, if I hated him. I try and shake down the irritation I am feeling with him this evening, and tell myself it's unfair. It's not his fault, I think, perhaps he doesn't even see it yet. It is just about possible, I suppose, that he doesn't see it yet.

He comes out into the dining room just as I'm shaking the tiles into the bag.

'Do you want to do something for your graduation?'

I weigh up how to respond to this opening. It's a gesture, but not enough of one to be significant. He wants to have sex, I think.

'We can do – it's not a big deal though. I mean, I had my proper graduation years ago, didn't I? I was only doing this for the course itself – I don't really care about the degree.'

I've acknowledged the gesture, but I have not overly committed myself. It's not that I don't want to have sex with him, but it's not that I do either. I'm not going to end up feeling good about it either way.

He falls asleep on the sofa, and I go up to bed before him. When he comes up, he puts his arm around me, and I pretend to be asleep. He sighs, turns over. I wonder now if it would even be possible to make things work in that way between us again. I could pretend, I suppose, and maybe if I pretended enough it would end up working in the end anyway. Isn't that what we're supposed to do, to keep things fresh? Make time, even when you're busy. Make an effort, even when you're tired. Care, even when you couldn't care less. Get dressed up, go on date nights. At what point do you just give up though? Because we're told that too, aren't we? Know when to quit. Try to make it work for the sake of the kids, but not only for the sake of the kids. Damage them if you split up, damage them if you don't, damage them either way.

I think about what it was like in the beginning, when we would have had sex every night, more than every night. And I think about what it was like after Max was born, before I started the business, and I used to worry about Dan finding someone else. I still think maybe he did, perhaps more than once. It was the not knowing that used to drive me mad – the feeling of suspicion but never knowing if it was justified or not. Whole scenarios imagined to the point of realisation. Trust your gut, but don't trust your gut.

But when I think about him finding someone else now, it is imbued with an overwhelming sense of relief. I can imagine myself even being philosophical about it.

'It's ok,' I can hear myself saying. 'I know things haven't been working between us for a while, and you must have been lonely. But obviously we can't go back now, not now that it's happened.'

I will be like an actor in a drama, playing a part I have scripted for myself, empathetic and yet uncompromising, shaping an affectation of words to mask a predetermined outcome.

I would have to be the one to leave though, to take action, even if he gave me no choice. He must be just as disappointed in me as I am in him, but he has always been so complacent. It is the thing that has always irritated me the most about him. I knew a therapist once who used to say 'The way you do anything is the way you do everything' and it is certainly true of Dan. But I don't want to take responsibility for it either – I don't want to be the one to call it, to be the one to say, once and for all, that our marriage is over. The way you do anything is the way you do everything. Perhaps we are more similar than I care to admit. I don't hate him, but I do hate myself. I hate the person I have become, and I am bored of the person I have become

– not of Dan, not of family life, not really, but of the person it has turned me into. Of the person I have allowed it to turn me into.

As soon as they all leave the next morning, a jolt of nervous excitement runs through me. I couldn't have watched it last night, even if I had told Dan about it, but I can't hold out any longer. I don't even make coffee, just take what I need and bring it back upstairs with me. I sit under the covers, back against the headboard, laptop balanced on pulled up knees, and take a deep breath. I almost don't want to start it. I can't wait to see it and yet, at the same time, I don't want it to start because I don't want it to be over. I will never have this anticipation again. I will be able to watch it as many times as I like, but I will never be able to watch it again for the first time. I will never again have this feeling of wondering if it's worked, this feeling of hoping that it's worked. Like buying a lottery ticket but then not checking the numbers because, until you do, the possibility of winning is still alive. The gamble isn't really made until you check the outcome. I have always been fearful of narrowing possibilities, the closing of doors. It is the worst thing about getting old, the balance shifting between what could still happen and what now cannot ever happen; the gradual recalibration of what might remain until, eventually, only certainty does.

No one else will ever see it like this, I think. They will be able to, of course, but no one will. No one else is going to sit there in that gallery and watch the whole two hours like this. There are bound to be one or two critics who will watch it all the way through, for sure, but they'll be taking notes and thinking about their interpretation, their 'take'. No one else is ever going to watch it the way I will. No one else is ever going to see it the way I will. And, I can't deny this is the thrill, no one else is ever going to see him the way that I am going to see him now. There will be a part of his life, a part of him, that only existed for me. It is the most wildly narcissistic thought I have ever had in my life.

I watch it all the way through, without a break. At first, he is conscious of the camera, just like I knew he would be – just like anyone would be. He is adjusting both physically and emotionally to the task in hand, wrapping his body and mind around what is required of him. He takes a deep breath, starts to relax, and then visibly begins to settle. You can see that the thoughts are running, but that he's probably just cycling through surface level stuff. Then something else creeps in, a hint of boredom, I think. He starts to act – not overdoing it or anything, just a little bit below the surface. Oh god, I really hope he hasn't done this all the way through or it won't have worked. But then he smiles his caught-out smile and shakes his head just a little, eyes straight to camera. It's for me. He's remembering, I think – he's remembered what I said about not acting. My cheeks flush, and something flips over inside. I realise that I am grinning back at him as if he can see me. He runs his hands through his hair in the way that he always does when he's being interviewed, when he's thinking, or stalling, or just a bit self-conscious for a moment, and then, thank goodness, his thoughts turn inwards again.

And then it works – it really works. I start to think, perhaps for the first time, that maybe Karl is right. Maybe this will change my life after all, maybe this is it for me now. Most of the time after that his facial movements are slight, a twitching of the lips, the moistening of an eye, the trace of a frown. Occasionally there's more though, and those are the moments that keep you watching. It's eerily hypnotic, the intimacy of it being just him and the camera, just him and the viewer, just him and me. Each time he moves his head slightly, his eyes appear to change colour – ranging from blue, grey, green, all the way through to amber. It's to do with how the light falls ever-so-slightly differently on the irises according to each miniscule change of position. I have always thought that his eyes must be naturally blue because of this, because of their capacity to seemingly appear so different depending on the photograph (blue is the most likely colour for this phenomenon to occur), but I have never been able to determine their exact shade before, and I feel a tug of regret that I wasn't brave enough to look properly when I had the chance yesterday. I would have liked to have seen them, really seen them, just once. If you listen carefully, you can hear his breathing. I find myself subconsciously synchronising mine with his, deepening the spell. You can almost believe that, if you listened hard enough, you might even be able to hear his heartbeat.

At last it is over, it is done, and there it is – my tiny glint of extraordinary. The moment where James Talisker existed in this world only for me. I sit there for a long time afterwards, not quite stunned, but spaced out, just floating around somewhere in the space between thought and feeling. And, after a while, I find that I do feel different somehow after all, something has changed in me after all, because that tiny glint of extraordinary exists inside of me now – I have internalised it. I had been worried, perhaps hoped, that this crazy trajectory I was on might have all just started and ended with James Talisker, that I was just some kind of super-stalker after all. But now that it's over it doesn't matter that I will never see him again. What matters is that there is a part of me, even if only a tiny part, that made this happen. A part of me that is active now, and will want out again – a part that won't be kept inside any longer. The poles are beginning to shift, and I don't yet know how long it will take, or how much devastation it will cause, but it will turn everything upside down in the end. It has to, because it has already started, and it can't be overridden now. It's going to keep on making things happen, it's going to keep on making art.

THREE

I don't sit in on the first screening, but hover in the reception room outside instead. The film will run on a loop the whole time the gallery is open now, and some people have obviously decided to come for drinks first and view later – or perhaps they are only here for the drinks, or to be seen, anyway. I don't recognise anyone, and no one approaches me. Karl is coming, and several students from my year, but they're not here yet. I expect people will start drifting in from the screening soon – I can't imagine anyone is going to sit in there and watch the entire two-hour film tonight. Emily, from the gallery, will be here – and there are a few other people I've got to know while I've been in and out prepping the room and equipment. Catering staff are circulating with drinks and canapes, and I accept an offer of a glass of something fizzy. I caution myself to try and drink slowly. Some of the people in here will be critics – I would probably know their names, but not their faces. I should be networking, I know, but I just can't bring myself to do it. I've always been too awkward socially, always preferred a work environment to any other. Actual work, that is, not this kind of not quite work/not quite play hybrid. Work, but not work. It's strange really, given that I spend so much of my life at weddings – you'd think it would have improved my capacity for social function. But, if anything, I think it's actually lessened it. Proximity to competence has only served to further highlight my own inadequacies. The room is starting to fill up, and I notice a few photographers dotted around now, starting to line up shots with who I'm assuming must be the most interesting people in here – they must have all been in the installation before.

I see the buzz of excitement first, over by the door. It starts there and then seems to radiate outwards, so that the whole atmosphere of the room lifts an octave. I know it's him even before I can see it is. I can't explain it, even to myself, it's like something smashes into me inside, a boom to the solar plexus that is felt before it is registered. People are already closing in on him from every direction, and he's smiling awkwardly, scanning the room. My heart leaps in my chest, just at the moment before I know his eyes will meet mine. And then they do, and he smiles, at me, and rakes his fingers through his hair, and I cannot tell if it is because he was nervous or irritated before, but the movement seems to settle him somehow, and then seems to settle somewhere, undischarged, in me. He turns to say something to the woman he came in with, and starts to walk towards me. I anticipate about a minute to compose myself, as he negotiates a path through all the people that are angling to talk to him – pretty much everyone in here, it seems. But then I start to doubt that his focus is on me at all, and I think it might be like when you are watching a play and you are sure the actor is speaking only to you, making eye contact only with you, but then you realise that it is just an illusion and every other person in the audience feels exactly the same connection that you do. But then he is before me anyway, and it is not an illusion, and he does not continue on to the next person, and I have not composed myself at all. He doesn't say hello, he just smiles and runs his hand through his hair again, and waits for a while – perhaps for me to catch up with him, I think. He looks slightly flushed, and I wonder if he's a bit embarrassed by it all, by all of this. But then, why did he come?

'Why are you hiding?'

Ok, that's direct.

'I'm not hiding.'

He raises his eyebrows slightly, and shakes his head. Now I feel even more self-conscious than I already did before and, as I glance nervously around the room, I realise that all gazes return to us – to him. He's still looking at me, and I wonder how long he will leave it before he says something. It feels like the whole room is looking at him, looking at me, and I know I can't wait it out. I will have to say something myself.

'If I was hiding, I wasn't making a very good job of it, was I?'

'No – sorry about that.'

'It's ok. I'm glad you came. I appreciate it.'

'You appreciate it?'

'Yes, I was grateful to you anyway, for agreeing to take part. But you didn't have to come tonight – I appreciate it.'

'Why would I agree to do it, and then not come and see it after?'

'I don't know.'

He smiles, and shakes his head again. I don't know where to look. My eyes feel strange, not quite achy, but tired. It feels like there is something stuck under one of my eyelids, and I think maybe I ought to have taken some paracetamol before I came out. It's probably the start of a tension headache. I tell myself to act normal, just act normal, he's no better than you just because he looks the way he does. It makes me feel slightly resentful. He must know the effect he has – how hard would it be to just try and make it a bit easier for the people around him? But this is a ridiculous thought; he can hardly be held responsible for the luck of his genes any more than an unluckier person might be blamed for theirs. It's not his fault if other people react this way, if I react this way. I can feel my cheeks burning again.

'Are you ok, Kate?'

'Yes. No. Sorry. I'm just really nervous. You don't have to stay with me – I'm fine.'

'It's ok, I'm hiding too.'

This time it's my turn to smile, and shake my head. 'Really?'

'Yes, really. Although…'

'Although what?'

'Well, sometimes it's best just to get it over with.'

'Get what over with?'

'Oh, you know, all this.' He uses his arm to gesture around the room, in a sweeping motion. 'Then you can just get on with the rest of your day. Or try to anyway.'

'Except this is the rest of my day. This is probably the biggest thing that will happen to me all year, maybe even my whole life. I don't think it's really the same for me as it is for you.'

'Maybe.'

And then he looks at me in the strangest way, as if he's trying to figure something out and he might find the answer located somewhere behind my eyes. It feels too intense, for the moment, for this room. It just feels too intense full stop. Maybe my eyes seem odd from the outside too. I look at my feet, and then around the room, at the faces all looking at us, at him, and then there is nowhere left to look but back at him again. I feel like I'm on the edge of something, like the slightest thing would tip me over now, almost as if I might cry, a bit like when people get sensory overload, except it's not that, it's something else. I watch his lips form an unspoken word, or perhaps not even a word, just a sound, and then he gently places his hand just at the top of my arm, and it feels like he's attempting to steady me. He is steadying me. And I am so grateful to him then – not for agreeing to the project, or being here tonight, but just for that, just for holding me steady, or trying to, even if it would not last.

'Do you trust me?'

'Why?'

'Well, do you?'

'I don't know, it's a strange question. I suppose I would have to say 'yes' after putting you through all this, wouldn't I? Or maybe that's a reason not to trust you – I mean, you might hate me now.'

He laughs, and I wish again that I didn't have to descend into nonsense around him. It's ridiculous, I should be able to be perfectly comfortable around him, friendly, confident, maternal even. What I shouldn't be feeling like is a seventeen year old girl falling in love for the first time. I did not even feel like this when I was a seventeen year old girl falling in love for the first time.

'Ok, you ready?'

'Ready for what?'

He scans the room, until his eyes meet with one of the photographers. It's not hard to do, because they've all had one eye on him anyway, waiting for him to move on to someone interesting. And then he makes something like the charades sign for film, which would look ridiculous if anyone else did it, but coming from him is somehow ok, and then points to me. The photographer tilts his head in acknowledgement, to show he gets it, and makes his way over. It's ok at first because it's just the one photographer, but then the others all crowd round at once, and I don't know where to look or whether to smile or act serious. And my face feels awkward, like it's not really part of me. Someone has given James a glass too, and they're asking us to do things like raise our glasses, or look like you're chatting, or look this way, Kate, or put your arm round her, James. And then he does put his arm around me, and I look up at him and, for a moment, I don't want to look away again, and he's so close I can catch the scent he is wearing. There's a warmth and sweetness to it which is strangely comforting, but completely at odds with him, with this whole situation, and then there's also something underneath that probably shouldn't be legal. I feel an almost uncontrollable urge to lean in. I am completely out of my depth.

'Enough now?' he asks, and I nod. 'Ok guys, that's it for now.'

The flashing gradually dies away – it's not like there's much to see here anyway, and they start to recede, watching and waiting for him to move on.

'Thanks,' I say, 'I think.'

'You should be used to this.'

He's right, I should be. But I have always hated having my picture taken, even as a child. It's why I've chosen photography as a medium, I suppose, to keep myself the other side of the camera, the other side of the barrier, permanently. And then his attention seems to shift to something behind me, and I experience it as an absence that is out of all proportion to the situation. He inclines his head slightly, smiles a silent acknowledgement.

'Kate, I think your friends are here.'

I turn around to see Karl and the others hovering, waiting for me to notice them, and obviously not wanting to interrupt my moment.

'Sorry, I didn't realise you were here yet. God, I'm so pleased to see you all – it's all a bit, well, it's genuinely terrifying.'

'Thanks,' James smiles, tousling his hair, and everyone laughs.

He's not nervous this time, he's doing it for effect, there's a difference. I feel something like a little jumpy glow inside at the awareness he's doing this for my people, for me. It's almost touching, and I suddenly realise I'm just standing there grinning, like a complete idiot.

'Are you going to introduce us then?'

This throws me a bit. I mean, obviously they know who he is, and I was expecting him to move on now that he's done his bit.

'Yes, of course. Sorry. Everyone, this is James. James, this is Karl, my tutor, and Soph, Cara, Evie, Finn – we're all students at college together. This is – this is my final assessed piece.'

'You don't all want to film me, do you?'

They all laugh again at this.

'No, the rest of us are a bit more low-key,' smiles Evie. 'Kate's our only superstar.'

She says it without any hint of malice at all, and I love her for it. It's not even true anyway. If anything, I've been the one to blend into the background throughout the whole three years, happy just to bask in their youth and enthusiasm and sheer, unadulterated, talent. I can remember how I'd felt at the beginning, as the token mature student on the course, not just shy and out of my comfort zone, but also faintly ridiculous, but they had never even questioned it. They had always accepted me completely as one of them, even if I did not feel deserving of that acceptance myself. And I feel such a warmth towards them now, for being here. I don't have many friends, only the most persistent have really persevered over the years, but these kids feel like my tribe tonight, and I am grateful to them.

'Oh, I see Julie wants me to rescue her,' James says suddenly. 'I'll be right back.'

It's true. The woman he came in with has been completely surrounded the whole time we've been talking. I feel slightly guilty for monopolising him for so long.

Karl is the first to speak. 'Kate, it's brilliant, you must be so, so proud. You are, aren't you? Proud of yourself? Because you really ought to be. It's beautiful. I mean, he is beautiful, of course, but it's not only that – there's… there's just so much truth in it, it's almost painful to watch. Exquisitely painful, I concede, but painful nonetheless.'

'You're passing me then?'

'Well, that depends… Do you have his number?'

'I wouldn't mind his number,' laughs Soph. 'God damn, he's hot.'

'Oh Kate, he is, isn't he?' says Evie. 'I've always liked older men.'

I deliberately make eye contact with Karl and smile at this. He is about the same age as James. They all seem young to me, but it only occurs to me then that the age gap between me and Karl and James is smaller than it is between the two of them and these kids.

'I don't really see what all the fuss is about him myself,' is Cara's offering. 'I prefer my men a bit rougher round the edges.'

'Well, if you've quite finished objectifying him, he's coming back over.' Finn says this light-heartedly, but he does have a point – it wouldn't really be ok to talk about a woman in this way.

James has brought the woman he came in with over to us.

'So, Kate,' she says, after he has introduced her as his agent. 'Tell us – was it really all about the art, or do you just have a mum crush on James?'

It seems good humoured enough, at face value, but there's something underneath the words that makes me feel a bit embarrassed – for me, of course, but also perhaps for her.

'Honestly? A bit of both I think.'

Everyone laughs at this except James, and I wonder if my attempt at humour has embarrassed him too. I shoot him an apologetic look, and everyone laughs again.

'You are definitely not old enough to be my mum, Kate,' he says, but he's still not smiling and then no one is laughing and it all suddenly feels a bit intense and awkward again.

It is a relief when Emily, from the gallery, appears

and tells me I really need to be circulating a bit more.

'Come on,' she says. 'I'll take you round, there's really no need to be frightened. Literally everyone has fallen completely in love with it already.'

I tell the others I'll catch up with them after, and Julie it's 'lovely to meet' her, and barely manage what sounds like a fairly ungracious 'thanks again' to James Talisker. I can feel my cheeks burning as Emily steers me away, I think she might actually be holding me up.

'This is your night, Kate,' she says. 'Do try any enjoy it. Honestly, everyone really is loving the installation, and they're going to love you too. Just relax and be yourself, you need to get used to this, you know, you can't be a shrinking violet in the art world.'

She's right of course – I'm far too dowdy for all this – but there is a part of me that does want to get used to it. There's a part of me that asks 'why not me?' And at least while I'm trying to string two sentences together in front of the critics, I'm not going to be making an idiot of myself over James Talisker, am I?

I somehow manage to get through the next hour or so and, by then, most people have drifted out into the galleries. I find Karl and the others waiting for me in the entrance hall.

'James said to say goodbye,' is the first thing Evie says to me. 'I kind of got the impression he might have wanted to come with us actually, but his agent whisked him away.'

I don't know why I feel disappointed – an hour ago, I couldn't wait to get away from him.

'He said he'd email you,' Finn smiles.

'Email me?'

'Yeah, his agent looked horrified,' says Cara. 'She said 'Oh, you're not, are you, James?''

'She's probably worried I'll try and rope him into some other low-brow installation.'

'No, it's not that – apparently he's just a nightmare for sending long emails.'

I've read this, of course. I think it's mainly with directors though, and I can't imagine he wants to work with me on anything else.

'I think he likes you Kate,' Evie teases.

'If only…' I joke, and we head off to the restaurant.

For a moment, in the cab, I close my eyes and allow myself to imagine a reality in which it might be possible for him to like me in that way. A reality in which I'm not eleven years older than him (or ten years, in the two weeks between our birthdays, if I'm being strictly accurate about it). A reality in which I'm the same age, or preferably younger, and it's a different version of me entirely – not the me I was when I was actually younger, but a more beautiful, assured, successful me. The sort of person I have never been. Me, but not me.

FOUR

On the train home, I don't think about James at all. I think about Karl. He was so lovely to me tonight. He'd waited until the clamour and flurry of the group had died down a bit after dinner, and the conversation had inevitably splintered into twos and threes, and then he'd very quietly and discretely handed me an envelope under the table.

'It's your final course feedback, Kate,' he'd said. 'I'm going to add something in about tonight, now that I've seen it, of course, but I wanted to let you know just how exceptional I think your work is, even without tonight.'

He had paused for a moment then, as if unsure whether or not to continue.

'Do you remember when you first came to interview?'

Yes, of course I did. It was the scariest thing I've ever done in my life – scarier even than meeting James Talisker, I think. And it wasn't like I'd been professionally trained as a photographer either. I'd been a social worker before I had the boys. Photography had always been just a hobby before that. It was Dan who suggested I give the wedding photography a go. I think he'd quite liked it when I'd been on maternity leave, and his job had taken priority, so something that fitted round the children seemed ideal to him. He didn't pressurise me or anything – I wasn't much looking forward to going back to work after having Max anyway, and I'd always fantasised about earning a living doing something creative. I'd started off working virtually for free, covering weddings at the weekends and portraiture in the evenings. It was hard in the beginning – I'd always been used to splitting everything fifty-fifty with Dan before that – but it built up quickly enough and, even if I wasn't earning as much as before, we figured there wasn't much in it once we factored in what we were saving on childcare. I didn't even have a proper portfolio when I'd gone for my interview with Karl, all I had to take with me were all the unwanted wedding and portraiture shots. The shots that no one wanted to include in their 'package' but which were beautiful to me. A veiled frown, a glance of passing regret between estranged parents, the remnants of a buttonhole, plucked bare, on a white tablecloth. Luckily for me, Karl saw something in them too.

'I know you think I cut you some slack that day,' Karl had said, echoing my thoughts. 'That I felt sorry for you, or something, or that you deserved a chance, but it wasn't anything like that. It really wasn't. I was excited by those photos, Kate, and I wanted to see more of them. There was so much raw potential there, and I wanted to be the one to help you shape it – I was doing it for me, not you. It was ego that motivated me, not altruism. I want you to know that. You really are an outstanding talent, Kate – watching you grow and develop your work over the last few years has been one of the greatest privileges of my career to date, and this thing you've done with James Talisker is brilliant too, but – '

I'd interrupted him then, of course. I've always found it difficult to accept praise. 'Karl, you know all I did was literally set a camera up and let it roll.'

He'd shaken his head. 'And you know it's not about that, Kate, it's about the concept. If it hadn't been right, it wouldn't have worked. And, actually, to be fair to the gorgeous James, I'm not at all sure that he's just a pretty face after all. I don't think he would have agreed to it if he hadn't already known it would fly. Oh, I'm sure he likes to give the impression that it's all 'impro' or something, but he knows what he's doing really. He must say no to a hundred projects for every one he says yes to. But this isn't about him, it's about you. What I wanted to say was that this thing you've done is brilliant, Kate, but you need to keep going after this. You can't just go back to doing weddings – you need to take a jump now, use this as a springboard. Or you will always regret it. And I will too – I will take it personally, you know.'

It had taken me a moment to be able to speak. He'd read me so easily.

'You don't need to worry,' I'd said, eventually, more steadily than my feelings ought to have allowed. 'I had thought I might just go back to normal after this, I wasn't sure for a while but, watching that recording back the next day, I knew I couldn't. I can't really explain what it is that's changed in me, but it was something about making it happen, I think, something about me making it happen. It felt good – too good not to feel it again.'

He'd nodded then, seemingly reassured. 'I know you don't always get the most support at home, Kate.'

'It's not that bad. I'm in control of my own work.'

And it's true. Dan hadn't wanted me to sign up to the course in the first place, that much is fair – I was already making a decent living doing something creative, he'd thought, and that should be enough. But it wasn't enough, and I'd wanted more – even then. He'd never tried to stop me though. He may have been disapproving, but never overbearing. He is almost certainly still hoping that everything will go back to normal now, but he won't try and tell me what to do. He will be denigrating and sulky about it, but he would never presume to actually lay down the law over it. He wouldn't dare.

It's gone one by the time the train pulls into the station, and the house is in darkness when I get home. I still haven't told Dan about the installation, and I wonder again if anyone else will mention it. I make a coffee, even though it is much too late for this to be a good idea, and sit down on the sofa in the lounge to drink it. I won't be able to sleep anyway. I'll be running through every moment I spent with James Talisker tonight ad infinitum, reimagining again and again what has already happened. The clock on the mantlepiece is ticking and, after a while, it seems to change rhythm so that there is an extra tick every minute or so. I've never noticed it before, and perhaps I'm imagining it now – like when you repeat the same word over and over to yourself and, in the end, it makes no sense at all. I could still tell Dan. I could go upstairs and wake him up, and tell him about the whole thing. About how I'd got the idea, and written to James Talisker's agent. About how I'd not heard anything back for weeks but then, just as I'd written the whole thing off and hung it on the peg tagged 'embarrassment', the reply email had come through.

'Thank you for your kind offer. James would be delighted to accept. Please can you contact me asap to make the arrangements.'

How Karl had set me up with the gallery, and then everything else leading up to tonight – all those heady weeks of preparation. And he'll be surprised, of course, but surely just a little bit impressed, and perhaps he'll tell me 'well done.' And I'll say sorry for not telling him sooner, but he wouldn't have wanted to go to the launch anyway, and he will mumble some sort of agreement with this. And then he might say that he's sorry too, for not being very supportive before, and we'll both bend a bit, and it'll be like a fresh start for us. So, I sit there for a while, thinking about this different kind of reality for me and Dan, allowing myself to feel it – the look of it, the shape of it, this one where our marriage is not over but refreshed, renewed, stronger than ever, listening to the clock tick on the mantlepiece, anticipating the extra moment, the extra time, before it arrives. But, in the end, I do not wake him, just as I knew I would not. Instead, I creep into bed beside him, and lie there, eyes wide open, thinking about the next thing I will make after this. And when, eventually, my eyelids do close, auburn lights flicker behind.

FIVE

I wait for Dan and the boys to leave before I start work. I can't really settle this morning – there's a backlog of wedding enquiry emails to get through, and photos still to send out from the last two I've done. I think about updating my website – there's still nothing on there about the installation, and it's ridiculous that there isn't. There's no doubt it will be good for business, but I'm busy enough as it is. I could set up a new site, just for the art side of things, but that feels like a bit too much of an overwhelming task for this morning. I turn to the emails instead. The most recent is from Emily:

Kate,

Hope you had a good evening, and got back ok yesterday. The response to the installation has already been phenomenal. We'd really like to commission another one, perhaps two? Obviously, we wouldn't expect you to work for free. Can you call me asap to discuss please? I'm not sure if you have an agent yet, but really think you should sign with one if not. We'd also like to discuss merchandise, both for the James Talisker installation and for any future commissions, and an agent would be able to negotiate all of that for you.

Congratulations again!

Speak soon, Emily

I should ring her back straight away, but I need to let things settle in my mind a bit first. I hadn't even considered an agent before, but the thought of negotiating contracts myself makes me feel physically sick – I'm not even looking forward to just ringing Emily back for a chat about it all. Karl will help, I decide, and I ping him out a quick email to ask for his advice on finding an agent. Just as I'm about to pick up the phone to ring Emily, a new email pops up – James Talisker. I'm starting to feel jittery, as if I've drunk too much coffee, but I've only had one cup this morning so far.

Hi Kate,

Really good to see you again last night. I would have messaged sooner, but I had to wait to get your email address from Julie first. I don't think she wanted me emailing you in the middle of the night...

Can I have your number? I'd really like to stay in touch. I know it sounds weird, but I thought we could be friends?

James

I close my eyes, and try to compose my thoughts. None of this makes any sense. What would James Talisker want to be friends with someone like me for? I'm not that surprised he's emailed – I mean, he said he would – but the fact that he's done it so soon is unexpected. I'd thought, alright hoped, that he might drop me a polite line in a week or two to say 'thanks' or 'well done' or something and maybe, in my wildest fantasies, I might send back a clever kind of reply and we might strike up some sort of penpal like correspondence. Or, probably more likely, he would've just forgotten he'd ever said that, and I'd never hear from him again. I certainly wasn't expecting an email the next day with an overture of friendship. Who would even do something like that anyway? Someone who isn't accustomed to rejection, I suppose. But when I calm down a bit it seems quite refreshing for someone to just ask to be friends, and it makes me think that there have been times in my own life when I could have been bolder. Maybe I'd have more friends now if I had been. Maybe I'd be able to accept an offer of friendship from a famous actor without feeling so unworthy of it. Perhaps it's research for a part, I think, he's forgotten how ordinary people are and needs a reminder. This seems plausible, at least, it must be something like that. I spend an hour and ten minutes composing and deleting and composing and deleting a reply. And

I wonder what it would be like to be friends, to really be friends, with someone like James Talisker – not just someone like James Talisker, the actual James Talisker. I wonder how long it would take to get past the looks even, let alone my seeming inability to be able to string a sentence together around him. I haven't even managed to look him straight in the eye yet. Maybe he sees me as some kind of mother figure, or older sister figure at least. Most likely, he'll get bored of me soon anyway. I don't think for one moment of not giving him my number. I think I would find it hard to refuse him anything. In the end, I send a one-line reply:

Sure, it's 01314 960839. Kate.

I really need to ring Emily now, but my phone is already vibrating on the desk. I feel so hot, I can't even breathe properly, like I'm about to go into a fight or something.

'Hello, Kate Williams.'

'Kate, it's James.'

'Hi.'

'Hi.'

'I didn't realise you meant now.'

'Why, are you busy?'

'No, I just wasn't expecting you to ring right away.'

'What, since I'm playing it cool so far?'

I laugh. 'I'm not very interesting, you know.'

'That's ok, neither am I. What are you up to?'

'Emails…'

'Oh, yeah, of course you are. What's your next project?'

'I'm not sure yet – another installation maybe. I've got quite a lot of 'day job' stuff booked in though.'

'What's the day job?'

'Weddings, portraits, some commercial stuff – mostly weddings.'

'Do you like it?'

'Sort of – it's ok.'

'You should quit it if you don't like it.'

'I'm not saying I don't like it – I just like doing other work more.'

'You won't need to do it now.'

'Maybe…'

'You won't.'

'Well, I'm not going to let anyone down. I don't need to decide today.'

We've been talking about me for too long, it's making me feel uncomfortable.

'How about you? What are you working on?'

'I'm between projects, taking a break for a bit. I'll

be shooting again after Christmas.'

Ah, that's it then. He's just bored, looking for a bit of diversion. He wouldn't usually have time for all this. Oh god – Emily.

'James, sorry, I really need to make a call.'

'Of course. Can I ring you later?'

'Yes, if you like.'

'Would you like?'

'Yes.'

'Ok, then.'

'Ok.'

'Kate?'

'Yes.'

'Can we meet up sometime?'

'Yes, I'd like that.'

'I have to warn you though, it gets a bit weird sometimes, being friends with me.'

'I can imagine…'

'No, I don't just mean with me being weird – I mean things around me can get a bit weird.'

'I know what you mean.'

'It's only fair to let you know, that's all.'

'It's ok, I'm a grown-up.'

'Yeah, I'm still working on that one, I guess. I'll call

you then. Bye for now'

'Ok, bye.'

'Bye.'

This is getting ridiculous, I hang up before it gets any worse. I haven't had a conversation like this since I was a teenager.

Fortunately, Karl has rung back with some recommendations for agents while I've been on the phone. Right – Emily. As I wait for the call to go through, I realise I'm still grinning like a complete idiot, and consciously try and rearrange my face into something resembling professionalism.

I tell her I'm working on the agent situation, and she tells me they'd like to make a provisional offer to host the new installation.

'You'll still own the work, Kate,' she tells me. 'It's just to host it.'

The amount she offers is more than I've earnt in the last four years put together. I realise I won't have any problems finding an agent now.

'Any ideas on who you want to work with next?'

'I've got someone in mind,' I say. 'But I'll need to approach them first, and it took weeks before James Talisker's agent came back with an answer. And, to be honest, I'm not even sure it's something

I can really pull off again.'

'I don't think that will be a problem. We've already had people approaching us this morning, Kate – big names too. Just tell us who you want, and we'll get onto their people. If they say 'no' we can think again.'

'Amber Cross' I say, with no hesitation whatsoever, but without the slightest expectation she will agree to it.

When I come off the phone from Emily, there's already a text waiting from James 'Don't forget to save me – I don't want you mistaking me for a call centre'. I smile to myself, and get a little buzz in my chest as I store his number in my phone. He must be really bored, I think. Of course, I know this won't last, definitely not once he's filming again, but why not enjoy it while I can?

And it's such fun – this texting and calling, and sometimes emails. It really is like being a teenager again. He texts me to ask me what I'm cooking for dinner or what book I'm reading or music I'm listening too.

I ask him 'Don't you know any other everyday people? Are you using me as some kind of social experiment or something?'

One night he sends me a picture of himself attending an award ceremony. Every face in the background is one I recognise. He tells me he's texting from under the table and all I can think of is that, amongst all those people, all those shining stars, he's thinking of me. But the next day I google the pictures from the ceremony, and I see him with his arm around this actress or that model or director, each one intimidating in their perfection, just like him, and I wonder at what point exactly he did think of me, or even if he did. It seems inconceivable to me, so inconceivable, in fact, that I begin to actually doubt it. Perhaps it is a delusion – some kind of elaborate hallucination scaffolded by obsession in my psyche, like the mirage of an oasis in the desert.

I begin to wonder what it would be like to tell someone, but who would I tell, and who would even believe me anyway? I can scarcely believe it myself. So I hug the secret inwards, guarding it from the outside world, fearful of exposing both the truth and the lie of it. I wait for Dan to ask 'Who are you texting?' or 'Why are you on your phone all the time?' but he either doesn't notice or doesn't care, or perhaps there is nothing even there for him to observe in any case.

SIX

Sitting in the corridor waiting again, just like before, I can't believe she said yes – Amber Cross. I'd thought the gallery would wrap up the James Talisker installation before this new one opened, but they've decided to run them concurrently – alongside the third, when it's ready, to make up a kind of triptych. I need to keep an eye on the time, but I've got ages yet. There's a message from James: 'Where are you?'

I hesitate before sending a reply. I've not told him I'm in London today. He's been asking to meet up, but I've been putting it off. I didn't know it was possible to want something so badly and yet feel so terrified of it. I keep thinking maybe I'll just lose some weight before I see him – not too much, just a couple of pounds, or try and do something about my hair, or grow my nails. Nothing that would take too long, just a few weeks. But, even as these thoughts run in my mind, I know that it will make no difference. That I'm just postponing the inevitable. He wants me for a friend, not for the way I look, and nothing I can do to my appearance is going to change that, so why should it matter? It's just misplaced vanity. I suppose I'm worried he'll have had enough of me, that being friends with me will turn out to be a disappointment, once we've met up in real life again, and I don't want it to end yet. I don't want it to end at all.

'I'm at the gallery' I reply, finally, and put my phone to one side, swapping it for my laptop. I'm not used to having this many emails to deal with. It's a good spot to work – the gallery have sectioned off this part while we're filming. I'm not expecting anyone, so I don't notice him coming until he crouches down beside me to whisper 'surprise' in my ear. I nearly jump out of my skin.

'I can't believe you just did that,' I say. 'Why didn't you tell me you were here?'

He shrugs, and sits down in the chair next to me. 'I wanted to surprise you.'

'Well, it worked.'

'I knew you were here – I've been waiting just the other side of the door, watching you through the glass. If you'd said you were somewhere else, I would've left.'

He does his caught-out smile, and then he's grinning – really grinning.

'It's really good to see you' he says, running his hand through his hair.

'Well, it's good to see you too – if a little unexpected.' And I realise it's true. Even though I've been nervous about seeing him again, now that he's actually here it just feels amazing.

'Amber told me she was your next victim. I've been planning this all week.'

'Did you tell her you were coming?'

'Yes, she thought it would be fun, and I thought maybe we could all do something together after – like go for lunch or something. That's if you want to?'

'Ok. I mean it's surreal enough just the thought of being with you, let alone with Amber too. It's like some kind of mad dream. Next we'll be hand gliding or eating jelly in a lift or something'

'Well, we can ask the girl from the gallery too, if you like. Or we can make it just the two of us, if that makes you feel more comfortable?' He switches on everything for this, and I laugh.

'Stop acting,' I say. But he's still looking directly into my eyes, and I feel myself flush even though I know full well what he's doing. I hate myself for being so predictable.

'Don't let me disturb you.'

I smile, and put my laptop to one side. 'I think you already have.'

He's sitting so close we're almost touching. He's not doing it on purpose – the chairs are joined together in a row, underneath a window that runs the length of the corridor. I don't know where to look. I can't look directly at him, but I can't look away either. So I shift sideways on my seat as if to face him, but then turn to look out of the window instead. I regret it instantly – it seems so contrived, and I can't change position again already, so now I just have to sit here and do my best to try and act naturally. He smiles at me – I don't think he can fail to notice my discomfort – and turns around completely, kneeling up on the chair, to face the window too. Resting his chin on crossed arms, he pretends to study a group of tourists in the quad below, but he is still smiling.

'Do I make you nervous?'

'No. Ok, yes.'

'Why?'

'I think you know why.'

'What, because I'm famous?'

'Yes.' It is that, but it's not only that. 'No, it's not that. It's just something about you, the way you are, the way you look. I find it disconcerting.'

'Disconcerting?'

'Yes, I'm sure I'm not the only one.'

'Honestly?'

'Honestly.'

'Don't take this the wrong way… I don't really tend to hang out with normal people usually. It's too complicated. It's not that I don't want to – it's just easier to be around people who are already used to the crazy.'

I wonder what he's doing with me again then, what kind of game he's playing, but I let it go for now.

'You must know how people see you though – it can't just be normal people, even other people like you must get nervous around you.'

'Oh, you mean how I'm supposed to look? Well, there is that. Apparently, I'm the most beautiful man in the world – it's been scientifically proven, and everything.'

'I did see that. However, I can't help but think they didn't literally analyse the features of every single man in the world for that research.'

'Me neither. Anyway, it doesn't matter if they did. It's not how I see myself.'

I can't help but raise an eyebrow at this.

'It's true, I don't. Why, do you think I should?'

'I don't know. You are objectively the most physically attractive person I have ever met, or am ever likely to meet, in my life, even if it isn't technically scientifically proven – so, yes, I suppose.'

Still resting on his arms, he tilts his head to one side to face me again. 'I do kind of want you to see me that way though. I know it's shallow, but I do. There's something about you that just makes me want to be real around you – I don't want to pretend I don't care when I do. Even though I don't normally. Care, that is. And I want you to be real with me too – I don't want you to be nervous around me. Or maybe I do, actually, if I'm honest – a bit. I don't know.'

I turn from the window and look at him then, really look at him. I look straight into his eyes, and force myself not to flinch or break my gaze at all. As it happens, his eyes are not blue, as I had hypothesised, or green, as others have speculated, but grey, with amber flecks around the pupils. It feels like an irrelevancy now. I wanted to see into him and, now that I am, he is perhaps not so unreachable after all. So we just sit there, facing one another, staring into one another like that, for what could be hours or could be minutes – I don't know. It's like I'm trying to desensitise myself from the way he looks, in the same way that someone with a fear of heights might climb an inch or so higher each time. And I realise that it's just about possible to withstand the vertigo because, although each of his features is undoubtedly beautiful – the eyes, the cheekbones, the hair, the jawline, especially the jawline – it's the sum of them all that's so intoxicating. So I am just about able to look into his eyes and forget about the rest for a moment, maybe only for this moment, but it is a moment nonetheless. And I also realise that this is something I want to do, because I want to be real with him too. Just as with the most intense aversion, this is something I'm going to have to overcome if I want to let him know me, and I don't think I have ever wanted to let anyone know me more. I have never wanted anyone to know me more. I have never wanted anyone to know me and accept me more, to want me more. It is a moment that seems to stretch into eternity, like entering a black hole might feel if you could survive it, as if I could survive this anyway. I half expect to look out of the window again and it will be dark, with all the disorientation that follows a matinee showing. But it is not like that. I am coming to from something; a dream, but it is still daylight outside after all, and my mind is clear, uncluttered, relaxed – and it is me that eventually breaks the silence.

'I think it must almost be time for me to rescue Amber.'

'Ok, I'll wait.'

She doesn't jump when I open the door, just smiles. The energy in here feels completely different to how it did after James's recording.

'How was it?' I ask her.

'It was ok,' she says. 'I actually found it quite relaxing. I feel really chilled now.'

I smile. 'Good. I can't wait to watch it back.'

She doesn't come over and start fiddling with my stuff like James did. She just carries on sitting there for a moment, quietly observing me tidying everything away. There's a watchfulness about her that makes me feel seen in a way that I never usually do. I realise I like her. I like her a lot.

'James Talisker is outside by the way.'

'Ah yes, of course, the lovely James.' Her eyes glitter as she says this, and I feel like she's teasing me a little, but I'm not quite sure how.

'So, tell me, are you as in love with him as everyone else?' she asks.

'Irrevocably. Are you?'

'Me? Oh, god, no. I mean, I love him dearly, we're good mates actually. But I'm not at all 'in love' with him. He's not my type at all.'

I can see that she means it, she's not just saying it. I suppose, like James, she can have her pick of whoever she chooses. If he really is the most beautiful man in the world, she must surely be up there as at least one of the most beautiful women. That's not why I asked for her though. It was her voice, of course – I wanted to see what was behind it.

By the time we come out, Emily has arrived and appears to be chatting comfortably with James – sitting exactly where I was before. I feel a flicker of envy for the confidence her youth gives her, for how she can sit there so easily with him. I'm not really sure how to juggle all these people together, so I step back for a moment and wait for someone else to take charge. In the end, it is Emily.

'So, James tells me you're going for lunch. Of course, you're more than welcome to use the member's bar, if you want to avoid the crowds. It's usually pretty quiet on a weekday.'

Amber looks from James to me and then back to James again.

'Actually, sorry, I don't think I can make it after all – I need to get to an interview. I've got a car waiting if you two want me to drop you somewhere though?'

'It's ok,' says James, and a look passes between them. 'I've got one outside.'

'Really? You never use a car.'

He shrugs. 'The member's bar sounds good to me. Kate?'

I nod. I'm not quite sure how we've got to this point. I look to Emily, and James follows my gaze.

'Emily, you'll come too, won't you?'

'Sadly, no,' she says. I can see from her face that she genuinely doesn't want to say no to him. 'I have a meeting I really can't get out of this afternoon, unfortunately. I'll show you the way though.'

James carries my cases for me, and I let him, even though it makes me feel self-conscious and embarrassed, and we say goodbye to Amber at reception on the way.

'It's been so lovely to meet you Kate, a real honour,' she says. 'Let's do lunch another time, shall we? Just the two of us.'

She glances over at James as she says this, and he looks a bit sheepishly at his feet, but not before I notice the caught-out smile. I don't really want to think about whatever it is that's going on between them.

'I'd really like that' I say, and actually I find that I would. Spending time with James must be doing something for my confidence after all, I think. The thought of a lunch date with Amber Cross would have thrown me into a complete panic before, but now it actually feels like fun, exciting, the sort of prize you might win in a competition in your wildest dreams.

Emily reluctantly deposits us at the member's bar, and then we are once again alone.

'Shall we sit outside?' I ask. It looks quieter out there, on the balcony, and I imagine he probably likes to keep a low profile.

'Perfect' he smiles.

Someone comes to take our order quickly, and I walk over to the barrier to take in the view while we wait for our drinks to arrive. It's breezy up here, I could have done with a coat.

'Here,' says James, and he drapes the hoody he's been wearing over his shirt around my shoulders.

'Now you'll be cold,' I say.

'I'm fine. We can always go in if it gets too bad.'

'I wasn't sure if you'd want to sit in there,' I say. 'You must get a lot of attention.'

'You have no idea. I'm used to it though, you're not.'

I glance back inside, and I see that people are already staring. Now that he's taken his hoody off, he looks every inch the movie star, standing there on that balcony. Blue shirt, unbuttoned top, bottom, cuffs. Hair ruffled by the wind, and by his hand, always his left hand. He couldn't blend in if he tried. But there's something else too. He seems vulnerable somehow, exposed, and I feel an almost overwhelming urge to hug him, to look after him.

Having to eat lunch in front of him is a whole new level of torture, but I manage to force down about half a panini in tiny mouthfuls.

'Tell me about you,' he says. 'I want to know everything about you.'

'Well… I'm forty-five, married (to Dan), two kids – boys (Max and Josh). Max is 17, Josh 14. I used to be a social worker before I had them – photography was just a hobby before that, I started doing weddings and portraiture after having the boys, and just never went back to work properly. I've just finished my art degree, which I started three years ago. This is the first time I've ever had work exhibited, but I think you know that. What about you? Tell me something I couldn't read on the internet.'

'Well… there's the stuff you *can* read on the internet – 34 year old actor slash model, dabbles in music a bit. I sometimes wonder what I would have done if I hadn't got into acting – I didn't really plan it and I still hadn't even really thought about what I wanted to do with my life when it all started. Something you couldn't read about me on the internet is I have a degree in philosophy. I did it on the OU. Actually I've never told anyone that, other than my parents and my sister.'

'Philosophy?'

'Yep, since I was already doing the most useless job in the world, I figured I might as well take the most useless subject.'

'You don't really think that.'

'No, you're right – I don't.'

I don't ask him about his girlfriend. I know he has one, that they live together even, and I wonder why he doesn't mention her. Perhaps I suspect why, but I do not dare to think it.

After a while, the bar inside empties, and we agree to go in. We find a corner to huddle into and order some coffees.

'We could get a proper drink?' he suggests.

For a moment it almost seems tempting, but I remember I'm supposed to be working.

'Another time,' I say. The sky is starting to darken a little – we must have been here all afternoon.

'I need to get back,' I say. 'It's getting late. I've kept you far too long as it is.'

'Let me drop you home then. I've got a car waiting outside.'

'Thanks, but the train's fine.'

'Oh yeah, I'm sure it will be great fun with all these cases at rush hour, but I'd still much rather drop you.'

'I can't let you drop me – it's a three hour round trip, at least. The train will be quicker.'

I've hardly thought about Dan all day, but I think about him now. I can imagine James asking 'Aren't you going to invite me in? Introduce me?' and then the sheer awkwardness of Dan's absolute shock and James's realisation that I haven't even told my family about the installation, let alone about meeting him. Even if he just dropped me, and left straight away, how would I explain away being chauffeured home by a car and driver? I think about another reality, one in which I've told them all about the installation, where I could invite James in, and he could sit in our lounge, on our sofa, making small talk with Dan, over a beer, like a normal person I've just brought back from work. And the boys would be shy at first but they'd gradually creep down from their rooms to see what was going on downstairs anyway, and they'd exchange glances that would seem to say 'What's mum done now?'

'Come on, Kate, don't make me force you.'

'No, honestly – I really don't want you to. I'm not just being polite – I really don't want you to.'

He actually looks a bit hurt for a moment, but then he seems to detect something of my panic, so he shakes his head and lets it go.

'You could drop me at the station though?' I offer. 'Either the underground or the mainline is fine. I won't have to carry the cases too far then anyway.'

'The mainline then.' It's a compromise at least.

We leave via the back entrance and, just as promised, the car is waiting. We climb into the back seat and James asks the driver to take us to Liverpool Street. I feel self-conscious again in the car and, even though there is a screen between us and the driver, I'm reluctant to talk much. I cannot help but wonder what the driver is thinking – I must make an unlikely companion for a movie star.

I'm looking out of the window, watching the lights of the river slip behind, so I feel rather than see him take my hand. He gently pulls it to the space between us, and I turn to look at him. He smiles, and squeezes my hand just a little, and I can't remember the last time anybody looked at me that way. I'm not sure anybody has ever looked at me that way. For some inexplicable reason, my eyes moisten slightly with tears, and I turn back to the window so that he doesn't see. But I do not pull my hand away. As we gradually wind our way through the rush hour traffic, he starts to slowly stroke the back of my hand with his thumb, back and forth, just a fraction. Just a few millimetres each time, so that it barely even registers. It feels almost licentiously intimate. It is as much as I can do not to sigh.

SEVEN

'What's with the hoodie?'

I had forgotten I was wearing it, and I realise it must look ridiculous on me, given the height difference between me and James.

'It's Finn's.'

'I thought you were finished with college.'

'I am. He's got an exhibition coming up. I'm helping.'

It's not a surprise to me how easily I can lie to him. Perhaps it would have been once.

'You've been in town then?'

'Yes.' I feel a need to change the subject. 'You haven't forgotten I'm away tomorrow and Saturday, have you?'

'Well, I had, but it's fine.'

'It's on the calendar – Kent.'

'Yeah, I know, I remember now. Kate, mum was asking about us going out there for a few days after Christmas...'

I don't think I can do it, fly to Sweden with Dan and

the boys, and pretend that everything is normal.

'I don't think I'll be able to. I've got a wedding. Why don't you go though? Take the boys. I'll be away for a few days anyway.'

'A few days?'

'It's in Wales – Pembrokeshire.' It's the first place I think of.

I've been looking forward to the Kent trip, and I drive down early to get the most out of the hotel. Tomorrow's going to be full on – from photos with the bride first thing, and then all the way through to the evening reception – so I want to get a good night's sleep. I don't mind though – I always enjoy the driving time when I'm working away, and it's also quite a relief just to be doing something normal. The first few times I stayed away on my own, I hated it – it left me feeling empty somehow, being in a hotel room alone. But I soon came to enjoy the emptiness, to savour it. It's more about the simplicity of it than the aloneness. The lack of physical and emotional clutter around me seems to work on the internal clutter too. I love the clarity of purpose – to only have myself and my work to worry about. I don't phone home – I always used to when the boys were younger, but rarely do now, unless one of them seems miserable about something. Dan won't call unless he needs me for something. I check my phone one last time before

I go to sleep to see if there's a message from James. There isn't. I could message him, I think, but I won't. I realise I've come to expect his almost daily calls and texts, but maybe that will all die off now that we have actually met up again in real life. I don't want to think about it tonight, I want to keep a clear head for tomorrow, I don't want to think about how quickly I have got used to having him in my life, about how much I look forward to those momentary flashes of light in my day, I especially don't want to think about how I will feel without it, when it's all gone away, without him.

I check to make sure my phone is on vibrate before I go into the bride's mother's house early Saturday morning, and I see there's a message I've missed from James after all. At first I think it must be from this morning, but then I realise it was from last night, after I'd already fallen asleep. I send him a quick 'sorry, only just seen this – working today' and then try to put him out of my mind, but I can't help sitting there and grinning to myself for a full minute before I get out of the car. And every time my mind drifts during the day, it is to the thought that he's not bored of me yet. I'll text him back tonight, I think, when I finish, even if he doesn't message me first, I'll text him.

It's an easy wedding today, for a change, so I'm

able to relax and enjoy it a bit. There's usually at least one set of divorced parents and new partners to accommodate in the formal photos, and various other family dynamics to negotiate. Parents who have somehow managed to safely deliver their children to adulthood with their own relationship still intact often mistakenly assume that, by the time the children of their less self-satisfied contemporaries grow up and get married, all previous feuds and embitterments will have been, if not quite resolved, at least blunted – but that is rarely ever the case. It is much more likely for old resentments simply to have been held in stasis for many years, only to erupt in an atmosphere charged by the heightened expectations of happiness that a wedding inevitably triggers. But there are no such difficulties to be sensible of today – this is a happy, confident couple with two sets of happy, confident parents, and the only real concern of anyone is whether or not the bride's father will be able to make it all the way through his speech without crying too much. The sun is shining, and that autumn foliage is going to look stunning in the background, so my job is made even easier still. They've asked for informal shots too, and I stay for the evening. I make sure I capture the arriving guests, as well as the principals letting their hair down. I should be able to get away by about ten, I think. There's no expectation to stay to the end – the couple are staying in the hotel, as are most of the guests, so there's no departing line or car to worry about.

My thoughts are interrupted by the groom's brother.

'Hi, it's Kate isn't it? Can I get you a drink or something? You must be shattered.'

'Hi. I'm fine, thanks. Actually, I'm nearly finished. It's been a lovely day, hasn't it?'

'It has. I'm Jack, by the way. Are you sure I can't get you anything before you go?'

I smile, and shake my head. He seems nice, and he's been watching me on and off all day – well, since the first group shots anyway. He's older than the groom, but not by much. His hair is greying, though still mainly dark, and his face, if a little weather beaten, is creased in all the right places. He looks outdoorsy, in a relaxed kind of way, the sort of man you could go fell walking or kayaking with. I feel flattered to be noticed by him and, if I'm honest, a bit grateful too – it doesn't happen all that often.

'No, honestly, it's fine. I'm all done. I won't disturb the happy couple – could you just tell them I said I'll get everything sent over next week? It should all be there waiting for them when they get back.'

'Of course, and thank you so much on their behalf – you've been brilliant.'

'Well, wait 'til you see the photos first.'

'Are you staying in the hotel?'

'No, I'm booked in just down the road. I don't like to take up guest spaces.'

'Let me give you a hand out with all your gear then?'

'That would be great, thanks.'

He waits until we get to the car to ask for my number, and I politely tell him thanks but I'm married, and add a 'happily' on the end, with a smile. He takes it well, as I knew he would, and we part with a 'lovely to meet you' and that's the end of it – but I run it through my mind again on the drive back to my hotel. It's not the first time something like this has happened – emotions do run high at weddings, after all, but I've never really felt tempted before. I'm not tempted now either, but I can't help feeling that I might have been if it wasn't for this thing, whatever it is, this thing with James.

Back at the hotel, I don't have to message James first because there's already a text and a missed call from him.

I reply to his 'you finished yet?' text from five hours ago with a 'yep, just finished.'

The phone rings almost straight away.

'Kate, are you ok?'

'Yes, fine, I've been doing a wedding. How are you?'

'I'm fine too. I was worried about you.'

'Oh, sorry. I often stay for the evening – if they want me to.' I don't know why I'm apologising – I haven't done anything wrong. I'm irritated at myself now.

'That's ok. I'm glad you're done now – I missed talking to you yesterday. It feels like I haven't seen you for ages.'

'It's been two days…'

'I know. Where are you?'

'Kent.'

'Whereabouts in Kent?'

'Canterbury.'

'Are you on your own?'

'Yes, I always go on my own.'

'Can I come over?'

'Sorry – what?'

'Can I come over? If you're in a hotel, that is. Can I come over and stay?'

'Ok… that's a bit forward… I'm probably just going to go to sleep soon anyway, to be honest. I'm not sure I'll be much company.'

'I'm not going to try anything on, if that's what you're worried about, I promise – I just want to see you. I'm only down the road, at my parents – my sister can drop me.'

'Ok, yes then, I suppose – sure.'

After I hang up, I sit there for a minute or two, heart racing. I don't know what's going on here, there's no frame of reference. I tell myself it's fine, that he doesn't want me that way, but then I wonder what way he does want me. And what if I want him in a different way, in a way that I can't ever have him? What if I want him in every way?

He texts me when he's outside, and I go down to let him in. There's a car waiting with the engine running, lights on, and he waves to tell them to go when he sees me coming. I catch a glimpse of cornsilk hair, pale face, as she drives off. Does she look... worried? It almost makes me want to laugh out loud, the thought that James might come to harm in this situation, when I am the one taking all of the risk. As if he has anything at all to fear from me.

He kisses me on the cheek and says 'Hi.' I'm conscious of the girl on the desk watching us through the window and I'm relieved when he pulls the collar up on his coat so that we can get past her without her realising who it is I'm trying to sneak in.

We don't speak until we get to the room.

He gestures to the holdall he's been carrying 'I snuck us out a nightcap. My dad's favourite malt – don't know if it's any good.'

He passes me the bottle and I pour us each a measure in the coffee cups. It smells like tobacco and, when I take a sip, it burns like ash. I've never tasted anything like it. We sit facing one another, me perched on the edge of the bed, him on the sofa bed opposite.

'What are we doing here?' I ask.

'I don't know.'

'Didn't your parents think it was weird you leaving in the middle of the night like that?'

'I told them I was going to a party I'd forgotten about.'

'Your sister then.'

'I already told her about you.'

'What did you tell her?'

He smiles. 'It doesn't matter – she knows it's hard for me to have normal relationships, she worries about me, I think.'

I nod. 'She looked worried,' I say.

I pour us both another whisky, and set the bottle down on the bedside table. Everything's starting to get a bit blurry round the edges, and I yawn.

'I'm sorry, I'm really tired. I did say I wasn't much company, didn't I?'

'Sleep then, if you need to, I don't mind. I only wanted to see you. I'm happy just being here.'

I shake my head, too tired now to try and make sense of it any more, and lie down on the bed facing him.

'I know this is weird,' he says. 'But I wasn't sure when we'd get an opportunity like this again.'

There is a pause, and I feel like something is expected of me, but I'm not quite sure what.

'Can I come over there?'

I nod, and shuffle over to the other side of the bed so that he can lie down beside me. There's only a few inches between us now, and I can breathe in the scent of him. It's all citrus and wood, and sweet burnt whisky.

He reaches out to take a curl of my hair and coils it round his finger. It pulls slightly on my scalp, and I feel a shiver in my brain.

'I meant what I said on the phone – I'm not going to do anything.'

'I know you won't.'

He smiles, and shakes his head. 'It's not that I don't want to, Kate. I just don't want to fuck this up.'

'I've never done anything like this before.'

'You think I have?'

'I don't know. I don't know what you want from me.'

'I don't know either. I can't explain it. It might be to do with the film, or even before maybe. Did you always know I'd say yes?'

'No. But I thought if anyone would say yes it would be you, and I never wanted anyone else anyway.'

'That was why I said yes. It felt like you'd seen something in me that other people hadn't.'

'I think other people see it too.'

'It felt like you'd seen something in me that other people hadn't, and you still wanted to see more. It wasn't like I was opening myself up to the camera, it was like I was opening myself up to you. You must have seen that?'

I nod. I can't deny it, I had seen it, when I'd watched it back I'd seen it.

'But afterwards, it was like a switch had been flicked. I wanted you to see all of me. I want you to see all of me now. I can't stop thinking about it, about you. And I want to see all of you too, I want you to let me. That's what I want from you. I don't know what this is but, whatever it is, I want it to be real.'

I don't know what to say, so I say something real.

'You're not like anyone I've ever met before.'

'I'm sorry. I'm being really intense, aren't I?'

'It's ok, I quite like it.' I do like it, it's exhilarating – like walking a cliff edge on a windy day.

'I'm not normally like this. I mean, I am normally like this, but not normally with other people. I don't know if it's you, or your mad project, but it's you either way.'

'I got the idea from you though. I didn't think up my mad project and then think of you. Thinking about you made me think of the project. I'm not saying I wouldn't have done it with someone else if you'd said no, but I wouldn't have got the idea in the first place if it hadn't been for you.' I smile, slightly surprised at my own candour, I must be really tired. 'And now I'm the one being intense.'

'There's something I should probably tell you, something I probably need to tell you – I knew you were going to be here tonight. That's why I went to my parents this weekend. You left your diary open at the gallery the other day. I know I shouldn't have looked.'

'No, you shouldn't. But then again, I probably shouldn't have spent even half the amount of time I did reading stuff about you on the internet.'

I can feel my skin reddening.

'After you met me?'

'No, it's worse – before. I'm not even joking. I'm ashamed of it now – I was ashamed of it then even. I was like a teenager.'

'It's ok, I'm glad you did. I wouldn't have met you otherwise, would I?'

'I'm basically a stalker.'

'Well, you wouldn't be the first…'

Or the last.

He holds out his hand to me, palm open. I take it, and we just lie like that quietly for a few minutes. My eyes begin to flicker shut. I don't want to fall asleep. I want to study his hair, summer shot through with autumn, dark and dirty against the stark white of the pillowcase. It would make a beautiful picture, I think. But my eyes close anyway.

We're still holding hands when I wake. I'm thirsty, but I don't want to move. I wish I hadn't fallen asleep so soon, it feels like such a waste. After a few minutes, his eyes flicker open too.

On the drive back to his parents' house, he seems subdued, and I think he's probably regretting accepting a lift from me, wishing he'd taken a cab instead. His anxiety not to be noticed this morning is prickling, putting me on edge too. I wonder why it would be so bad – it's not like anyone would see me as a romantic interest. They'd probably just assume I was a relative or staff or something. But then I remember a picture I'd seen of him online, just after I'd approached his agent. He'd been sitting in a hotel bar, just having a drink on his own, on a break from filming, the article had said. You could see his face was taut with anger, but you could also see how determined he was to pretend he hadn't noticed he was being photographed. Furiously studying his paper, like a child desperately trying to ignore taunts in the playground. I'd wondered how many thousands of photos, how many tiny intrusions, it had taken to get to that point. It was a form of bullying. And I'd felt a strange sort of protectiveness towards him then, even as I was complicit in his discomfort, and I realised it had to stop, I had to stop. I was feeding it all, I was culpable.

'Would you like to come in? You haven't had breakfast.'

'It's ok, I've had coffee – I'll stop at services.'

'Are you sure? They'd love to meet you. You can see my sister's curtain twitching already.'

I laugh. 'God no, the thought is terrifying. I dread to think what they'd make of all this.'

'They know about the installation – they've seen it. My mum watched it all apparently.'

Strange that he's told his family about me, and yet I've still not even mentioned him to mine.

'Honestly, I need to get back anyway.'

I wait for him to say goodbye, and get out of the car, to walk into his parents' house without a backward glance, to move away into the distance again, but he is waiting for something too, or considering something, weighing up variables perhaps in his mind. I tap my fingers self-consciously on the dashboard, and then wipe at the slight fuzz of dust that has collected there. When I turn to face him, he smiles, shakes his head, smiles again. He's nervous too, I think, and, at last, he speaks.

'I don't want you to go. I don't know when I'll see you again, if I'll see you again. It feels out of control.'

'How do you think I feel?'

He smiles at that.

'Fair, I suppose.'

He seems to make his mind up about something.

'Look, I've stayed in your hotel room now – will you come and stay with me in mine? Any night this week, or next – you choose. We can order in pizza, like a sleepover. I know it's weird, but it's less weird than if we try and do normal stuff. We won't be able to do normal stuff.'

And then the lightness in his tone gives way to intensity.

'We probably won't ever be able to do normal stuff, Kate. Nothing is ever normal with me.'

It doesn't occur to me that I might say no, or ask for something more. I'm not sure I can refuse him anything now.

EIGHT

The hotel is in Holborn, it's the sort of place I have only ever checked into a few times in my life before. He's made the booking in my name, and they ask for ID at the desk.

'Mr Talisker has already checked in,' the receptionist informs me. 'Would you like me to let him know you're here?'

'No, thank you, it's fine. I'll call him.'

She nods, and I wonder if this is a regular occurrence. My cheeks burn at the thought.

Upstairs in the suite, I sit down at the desk for a minute and check through the messages on my phone. I don't call him right away. I don't know why. It's a bit late to back out now.

The phone vibrates in my hand. 'Where are you?'

'I'm here.'

'I know, I heard you come in. I'm next door.'

'Ok, I'll be there in a sec.'

He opens the door as soon as I knock. It takes me a moment to take everything in. There's clothes everywhere, a laptop open on the desk, and what I think must be a pile of scripts scattered across the sofa alongside a guitar.

'I thought you lived in London,' I say, without thinking, then instantly regret it.

'I do. It's complicated.'

'Ok.'

'Actually, it's not complicated. I just don't want to talk about it. Not yet anyway.'

I nod. I get it. I don't think I want to hear it. And there are things I don't want to talk about either.

'Are you hungry? I've asked them to send up pizza, and wine. Lots of wine. Do you want anything else? My plan is to get you drunk, just so you know.'

'Pizza and wine is perfect. And I'm a bad drunk, just so you know. My jokes get worse and, apparently, I talk in a funny voice. What are you like when you're drunk?'

'Melancholy. But not with you, I don't think. I'll probably just act like an idiot instead.'

I push the scripts to one side, and sit down on the sofa. I'm really tempted to look, but I resist the urge. I've probably fangirled enough already.

The pizza is good, better than I expected from a hotel kitchen – even this one – and weirdly, in some strange way, it does almost feel a bit like a teen sleepover after all. Now that I'm learning how to loosen up a bit around him, I'm actually starting to enjoy it a whole lot more. It feels like... well, fun. And it's been so long since I've just had fun with someone, anyone, that it takes me a while to recognise it for what it is at first.

'What shall we do now?' he asks, after we've eaten. 'Shall we watch a film?'

'I'm not sure,' I say. 'It sounds like a test I will probably fail miserably at.'

'Not one of mine obviously – that would just be weird. What sort of thing do you like?'

'I don't know – all sorts of things.'

'Come on, what's your favourite film ever?'

That's easy. 'Pulp Fiction.'

'You like Tarantino then?'

'Yes, mostly, some more than others.'

'Do you think I should do a Tarantino?'

'I'm surprised you haven't.'

He laughs. 'I'm surprised I haven't. Maybe he doesn't rate me.'

He's slouched back on the bed, propped up against the pillows, and he spills some of his wine on his shirt when he laughs. He looks more relaxed too. I like to see him laugh, it changes his face completely. It still takes your breath away, but it's just not quite as intimidating as when he's serious.

'Why don't you come over here and we'll see what they've got?'

I prop up the pillows next to him, and sit cross legged on the bed with my back against them. This would have thrown me into a complete panic just a week ago, but it feels almost easy now.

'It could have been worse, I suppose – you might have wanted me to try Austen or something.'

'I don't know,' I say. 'I think you'd make a pretty good Wentworth.'

He laughs again. 'This isn't a Richard Curtis rom com – I'm not going to do Captain Wentworth just because you think I should.'

I turn to face him, with as deadpan an expression as I can manage. 'No, you're right,' I say. 'Tom Hardy would be the obvious choice for Wentworth anyway.'

'Tom Hardy? So, that's how it is, is it?'

'Well...'

And then the mood changes, unexpectedly, and he's not laughing anymore, and any ease I might have felt a moment ago dissipates into the air like a vapour. My breath catches in my throat, unable to reach my lungs. He swings over to kneel astride me, using his hands to support his weight on the headboard. He leans down so that our faces are almost touching.

'So, you wouldn't say no to Tom Hardy, but you'd say no to me?'

I know he's only acting, teasing, but it feels almost scary – like a cliff edge on a windy day again.

'And you'd do things with Tom Hardy that you wouldn't do with me?'

I'm smiling, but shivering inside. 'I'm sure Tom would be the perfect gentleman.'

He leans down further still, so that his hair falls across my cheek, and his lips brush against my ear.

'Maybe Tom wouldn't take no for an answer.'

'Perhaps he wouldn't need to.'

And then our breath seems to catch together on the same beat, and I wonder for just a fraction of a second if he's not really acting after all, if there's a part of him, even if only a tiny part, that wants me the same way I want him. The thought is maddening in its cruelty. But then he laughs, and I laugh, pushing him away, and it's all just a joke again.

We don't watch a film in the end, not that night. We listen to the radio, and talk about our lives as kids instead. We talk about our families and how they seem quite similar really. We talk about the age gap between us, and how I would have been starting secondary school the year that he was born. It makes me feel ancient.

'I suppose you Gen X-ers were all hardcore,' he jokes.

'Yeah, that's us – not like you snowflake millennials.'

I'm lying with my head on his chest, and he has his arm cradled round me. I've never been this intimate with anyone I've not been sleeping with before. It occurs to me that maybe this is an age thing, perhaps this is just how friends are nowadays.

'All my stuff's next door,' I say.

'Don't you want to stay with me?'

'I didn't think you wanted me to. I thought that was why you'd booked me my own room.'

'No, that's not why. I was hoping you wouldn't use it.'

'Why did you book it then?'

'So you wouldn't be embarrassed checking in, and so you'd have it if you wanted it.'

'I don't want it.'

'Maybe not tonight. You might want it another time though.'

'What makes you think there's going to be another time?'

'Isn't there?'

'Why would I want the room though?'

'You really want me to spell it out?'

'Yes.'

'I said I wouldn't try anything on, and I meant it – I told you I didn't want to fuck this up, and I don't. But I'm only human, Kate. I might cross a line you don't want me to cross. Maybe not tonight, but maybe one time.'

'Do you often cross those kinds of lines?'

'Is that your way of asking me if I've done this before? If I do this all the time?'

'I don't know. I'm not sure I want to know.'

'What do you think, Kate?'

'No, I don't think you do.'

I almost wish I didn't believe it. It would feel less riskier somehow, more charted, if I could trust him to know what he was doing, to navigate our way through this. There are no boundaries here, I think, no lines to cross, and it will take more than an empty hotel room to keep me safe.

NINE

Dan tells me he's booked to take the boys to Sweden on Boxing Day, so I book a cottage on the beach in Saundersfoot for the same week. I should feel guilty about not going with them, but I don't. I've never been away on my own before, except for work, and I wonder now why I haven't. I find myself dreaming up trips for the future, a future that does not include Dan. They'll still be holidays with the boys, of course, but then they'll also be times like this when they'll be with Dan and I'll be free to come and go as I please. Max will be at uni soon anyway, and Josh won't be too far behind. A new kind of optimism seems to filter into my thoughts in a way that I haven't experienced in years. But this is an optimism for a distant future, and one that can only exist after pain.

My trips into town become increasingly frequent, sometimes more than once a week. The days in between seem to pass by unnoticed, nothing more than a comma in a sentence. I think about him all the time, his face passing through my consciousness like a mantra. I drive myself near mad with fantasies that he feels the same way, that there is a connection between us that is somehow strong enough to survive the real world. But then, each time, I am overcome anew at the impossibility of it all. If he wasn't quite so successful, or quite so perfect, and I wasn't so much older, or so ordinary, if only the gap wasn't so wide and my feelings weren't so deep. I can't believe I have done this to myself, to allow myself to feel this way about someone I can never have. It's an act of self-harm that nothing in my life before now could ever have prepared me for, an act of self-harm I could never have even conceived of before. It's like when you stand on top of a tall building and you think to yourself that you might throw yourself off, but it's a safe thought because you know you would never actually do it. You are not that sort of person – maybe it would be a dangerous thought for someone else to have, but not for you. Except it turns out you are that sort of person after all, you always were, and you really did throw yourself off that building, and it can only end one way now.

Dan starts to stay out at night too. At first he attempts to provide cover stories, just as I did in the beginning, but then we find it is easier to simply give one another advance notice when we won't be back and leave it at that. Sometimes there is a clash, but one or other of us will find a way to reschedule our plans. There is never any resentment, no tallying of quid pro quo, just a polite, almost business like, tacit agreement to keep communications and questions to a minimum. We do not argue, there is no need. I know that this cannot go on indefinitely but, in the absence of any tension between us, the same kind of complacency that has always provided the bedrock of our marriage sets in.

When I look back at the twenty-six year old I was when I married Dan, I do not even recognise her. It had seemed like such a grown-up thing to do, back then, to settle down and start a family. I'd pushed for it even. A person could waste a lifetime, I'd thought, waiting for the perfect other to come along. So what if it wasn't love at first sight and mind blowing sex and everything music and movies told us it should be. Who ever really has that beyond the first few months anyway? We were good friends who had fun together and broadly shared the same values – that was enough, wasn't it? Except it wasn't enough – not really. It was enough to make a family, but it wasn't enough to make a marriage. And now all I see is waste – the lifetime I had been terrified of wasting, I have wasted anyway. It is the lack of imagination I find most incomprehensible now, that absolute failure to see the possibilities that might have existed beyond the known.

At night I dream of James. Dreams where we kiss as if the world might end, and dreams where mine does. Sometimes he is desperately in love with some other person and, for a meaning that eludes me, my subconscious is forcing me to witness it in all its technicolour glory. I want to scream and claw at his beautiful face, to bite into him, to make him suffer as I am suffering, but instead I smile and pretend to be his friend. Once I dream that we are in some kind of spacecraft, hurtling back to a crash landing on Earth. We know that we will die but we cling together anyway, to each cushion the other against the final moment. But the final moment never comes, something in us lives on, some small part of our consciousness survives the impact, and then I awaken, sobbing, momentarily wishing for a death beside him over a lifetime apart.

We meet at the hotel three days before Christmas. He had wanted to make it the day before Christmas Eve, but I find there is a line I cannot cross after all. I cannot choose to wake up in a hotel room with him on Christmas Eve when I could be waking up at home with Max and Josh. I do not explain it, I do not have to, I simply tell him I cannot make the day he has suggested.

The hotel have brought a tiny Nordmann Fir into his suite, and strung it with fairy lights. It seems a slightly strange thing for them to have done, since no similar tree has been placed next door.

'Don't you ever worry they might tell someone… about us, I mean?' I ask him.

'I'm a heavy tipper.'

He says this with a somewhat wry smile, and I cannot help but wonder how heavy. How heavy is the price of keeping this thing, whatever it is, a secret?

'I've got you a present,' I say. 'For Christmas.'

I feel a bit shy about it now, I almost wish I hadn't. It's an old cloth bound edition of 'Thus Spake Zarathustra' and it might seem as if I've put a bit too much effort into choosing it.

'I hope it's ok – I'm not that hot on philosophy.'

He seems genuinely delighted with it. 'It's perfect,' he says. 'Thank you.' He gives me a hug, and kisses me lightly on the cheek. The proximity and then immediate absence of him is almost painful.

'I got you something too, but won't I see you next week?'

'I'm away next week.'

His face seems to tighten slightly. 'With your family.'

'No, on my own. I've booked a week in Pembrokeshire.'

'What are you going to do?'

'I don't know. Sleep, read, walk, nothing exciting.'

'Why didn't you tell me?'

'I'm telling you now.'

'You know what I mean.'

I feel a snag of dissonance at his tone. On the one hand I find it slightly thrilling, on the other there's an undercurrent of control that doesn't sit well with me.

'You're not my dad.'

He looks visibly taken aback, sulky, as if he might cry almost. But then his face clears.

'Oh, god, Kate, I'm sorry. I'm being a complete dick, aren't I?'

'Well, yes, a bit, but it's ok, and you know you could come if you wanted to anyway.'

'Are you asking me?'

I shrug. 'If you like. I'd assumed you'd be with family or... well, you know...'

'I'd rather be with you.'

'I'm leaving Boxing Day though, and I'm not coming back until after New Year. I mean, I'll be away for New Year. I suppose you could come back sooner.'

'I wouldn't want to – it sounds perfect. Do you

want me to come though?'

I can't believe he needs to ask. 'Of course I do, you know that.'

'Will you ask me then? Properly? You never ask me – it's always me asking you.'

'I don't not ask you because I'm ambivalent – I just don't want to be presumptuous.'

'Ask me.'

'Ok, I'm asking you. Will you come to Pembrokeshire with me please? I'd really like you to.'

'Thank you, I'd love to.' Finally, he smiles. 'Your present can wait until Saturday then.'

I have become used to sleeping next to him now. We lie facing one another, arms entwined, drifting in and out of consciousness. Sometimes he will kiss my hair, my forehead, my lips and it is like being a teenager again, wanting and not wanting more. Whatever invisible line we have drawn, he does not cross it – his kisses are exquisitely light, delicate, chaste even. Almost unbearably so. I try not to think about it too much. I worry that my face or body will betray me in a way that there can be no going back from. I am not sure what would be worse – the almost inevitable rejection that would ensue, or the possibility of something else. Either way, the spell will be broken.

I awaken to find we have become separated in the night. He is sleeping on his back with his arm outstretched towards me. He murmurs something in his sleep that I cannot catch, and it lands as a feeling of dread in my chest. I remind myself again that I have no claim over him, not over his conscious mind, let alone his subconscious one, but there is no space for reason here. He murmurs the same word again, and then again once more. It is my name. I move closer towards him, I can just about make out the shape of him or imagine I can anyway. I reach out my hand, almost but not quite touching, tracing the outline of his hair, his cheek, his jawline. Features so sharp in my mind in the day seem to soften and merge at night. His eyes flicker open for a second, and he captures my wrist in his hand, pulling me closer towards him to rest my cheek on his chest. And I cannot stop myself in time, just the lightest brush of my lips where his heart must lie. A slight, sharp, sudden intake of breath and I feel rather than see his smile. I wait for him to go back to sleep and then, for the first time, I creep away from him to the empty room next door.

TEN

It is dark by the time we arrive at the cottage; the key has been left for us in a tin by the back door. The waves are close, and the scent of the sea envelops us as we unload the car. I feel as if I might wade right in and not even know it. The cottage is cluttered with the owner's books and trinkets, and smells of incense. A psychedelic yin yang throw has been used to disguise the threadbare sofa in the lounge, or perhaps to draw attention to it, and there are cushions everywhere – embroidered with elephants and stitched in sequins. There is a Buddha on the mantlepiece and, when we inspect the other rooms, we find a dreamcatcher suspended on the wall above the bed. It is like being in a 1970's camper van that has long since been parked up to rest but, somehow, all of the cliches seem to work together after all, and I think it is perhaps the most comforting building I have ever been in. They've left us a basket of wood and kindling for the wood burner, and James's enthusiasm is almost childlike as he sets a fire. I can't imagine he stays in places like this very often, and the thought makes me inexplicably happy. I lie down on the sofa for a moment, while he explores and starts unpacking the shopping. I've brought enough food and supplies to keep us going for a day or two. It's nice just lying here, listening to him rustling around, and I suddenly feel tired from the drive. After a few minutes he brings me a cup of tea, and sets it down on the floor beside me.

'I'll make us something to eat,' he says.

I sit up to drink my tea. I very rarely take it, but I like that he brought it to me without asking first, so I drink it anyway. It feels comforting. After I'm done with the dregs, I lie back down on the sofa again, and close my eyes. There is just something really soothing about this place, about being here with James, and I feel an overwhelming sense of calmness sweep over me. I can't remember the last time someone cooked for me, really cooked for me, and it makes me feel looked after in a way that I haven't been for years.

After dinner I tell him I'm tired and I'm going to bed. He still seems to be enjoying pottering around the cottage, so I leave him to it and, eventually, lulled to sleep alongside the occasional gentle creak of his movement, my head seems to hum with a happiness I do not feel quite deserving of and yet am unable to resist anyway. I wake up some time later, stirred by his weight shifting into the bed beside me, and, without even thinking about it, move closer into his arms. It's a strange feeling, this, to be so relaxed around him.

I wake up to sunlight, and the sound of James playing something on the guitar out in the lounge. I'd hoped I'd hear him play this week. He's murmuring some lyrics but his voice is too low to make them out properly. I keep still and close my eyes again, listening, sinking into the moment, pretending to still be asleep. I want to go in there so I can watch him too, but I'm frightened he'll stop if I do.

After a while, the pull is too great, and I find myself hovering in the doorway, waiting, until he looks up.

'Hey,' he smiles.

'Don't stop, I was enjoying it.'

I sit down on the sofa but, after a minute or so, he puts the guitar to one side.

'I don't think I can play with an audience.'

He's set the fire again, and I notice he's already made coffee. It's surreal being here with him like this, it feels like when me and Zoe used to play 'houses' as kids.

'Ready for your present now?' he asks.

'Of course.'

He hands me a small battered wooden box,

wrapped in tissue paper. The wood feels warm and smooth, softened by time. Inside is a sun compass, scratched but still working. It's beautiful, like finding a piece of buried treasure. I run my fingertip, gently, over the etched brass, as if I can absorb the memories of where it has travelled by doing so.

'Do you like it?' he asks, somewhat expectantly, but also slightly nervously, I think.

'I really do,' I say. 'It's beautiful. Thank you.'

'It's supposed to have been all the way to Antarctica, on one of the early expeditions. Well, that's what they told me in the shop anyway...' He smiles.

'I'd like to go there one day,' I say. 'I've always wanted to, ever since I was a kid. I'll take it with me when I do, then it will definitely have been there.'

'You know, I went there once years ago? With my parents – it was meant to be like our 'Disneyland'. I was sixteen. I used to creep out and sit on the deck on my own at night. It never got dark. It blew my mind, it was like being on another world. I can remember thinking that one day I'd meet someone and fall in love and, when I did, I'd go back and take her with me.'

His cheeks seem to flush slightly when he tells me this, but perhaps it is only the heat from the fire.

'And have you? Been back?'

'Not yet. I'd forgotten I'd ever even thought it – or, not forgotten exactly, just forgotten to remember, I suppose. I hadn't thought of it for years though – not until the day I met you, at the gallery. I hung around for ages after, just wandering round and round aimlessly, not really concentrating on anything, and then I was just looking out of the window, towards the river, and I saw someone get up from a bench and turn to look straight up at me. It was you. I knew it was you straight away. I don't think you saw me, but I felt embarrassed, like I'd been spying on you or something. And then I remembered Antarctica, just like that, and I wanted to take you, Kate. I'd still like to. We've never spoken about your family, you know, about your husband – '

'Let's not talk about it now.'

It feels disloyal to talk about Dan and the boys with him somehow. I can't even explain to myself why. I feel like I could do anything for him, would do anything for him, except that.

'I'm not going to make you. Look, I know there's stuff to work out, I know it's not as easy as just booking a ticket – or I would have. But something's happened to me with you – something different. It's like every time I think about something I want to do in the future now, you're in it. I can't help it, I can't stop myself. It's not just Antarctica, Kate.'

His eyes are searching mine, looking for something, for light maybe. It feels so intense. I know in this moment he wants me, but he's holding back, just like I'm holding back. He doesn't want to hurt me, I think. He cares about me enough to not want that. Perhaps he is as frightened of destroying me as I am of destroying myself.

'There's something else too. It's not a present, it's a silly thing – more like something I wanted to say really.'

He hands me a CD. It's printed with his name, a song title, some other details.

'It's a demo – my last one. I was trying to make a go of it before I got into acting, well I was kind of doing both for a while, I guess. I don't know how to say this without making it weird – like it could get any weirder – but it's like I was on this path, another path, which in theory wouldn't have led me anywhere near you or you to me, but I feel now like it would have done anyway. Like I might have kept on doing open mics, and you might have shown up one night, maybe you'd still be a social worker and be out for a drink with other social workers, you know, in the sort of place that social workers might go for a drink – or maybe I'd have done ok, and you'd still be doing what you're doing now, or what you were doing, and would have photographed me for something anyway, a local paper maybe. Or you'd be doing exactly what you're doing now, and would have had an exhibition somewhere, or at the same place, but with someone else, you know, me, but not me, but I'd still have seen you from the window that day. I don't know. I just feel like we would have met at some time anyway. Not like it was meant to be or fate or anything, just that some people's paths are bound to cross at some point whatever happens. And I still would have remembered Antarctica, that's the thing, wherever it was, whatever I was doing, or you were doing – I would have remembered that wherever I'd met you. It would have been the same, but not the same.'

He shakes his head, smiling, embarrassed, awkward but open.

'I know it sounds mad, I just wanted you to have it, like I'm just giving you something I would have given you anyway. You don't even have to listen to it if you don't want to.'

I trace his name and the song title on the CD with my finger, just as I did with the sun compass. I'm not sure I trust myself to speak. Meeting him even just once still feels impossible to me in this reality, this life, let alone in some other one. But I can't help wondering if it might have been different. If music was just something he did for fun, a break from the day job, and acting was something he'd only ever dreamt of. He would still be younger than me, still almost unbearably beautiful, but maybe I would have been brave enough to hope for something more in that reality – even if only for a moment. If his world had been smaller, more like mine, perhaps I might have tried to navigate it. But that's where he is right, I realise, it would have been the same after all – I'd have been lost in the end, just like I am lost now. It makes me think of something from a lifetime ago, from when I still was a social worker – the map is not the territory, we used to say. A truism borrowed from neuro-linguistic programming. It used to seem empowering then, the idea that the well-trodden track was not the only one worth pursuing, that there might be another path. But it seems to me now it works the other way too – the territory remains the same, and it is only the vantage point that changes. The compass might not always point North, but time will take you there in the end.

The beach is wide and beautiful. There are plenty of dog walkers and families about, but it's easy to keep our distance. He's pulled on a beanie and a scarf, and you can hardly see his face at all. It must be easier to hide in winter, I think. Occasionally someone will come within earshot with a cheery 'morning' and we quickly fall into a sequence of me grinning a 'hello' back and James just nodding a kind of silent acknowledgement. He never makes eye contact, but it's just enough not to appear rude. After a while, I almost begin to enjoy it, hiding in plain sight like this, and I can see it amuses him.

'I don't think you would like it so much if you had

to do it all the time, Kate,' he says.

'Luckily I don't have to then.'

'Do you think you could get used to it?'

I think about it for a moment.

'I don't know, is the honest answer. I think I'd be patient at first but then, yeah, I can see how it would really piss you off after a while.'

'It's why I don't hang out with normal people much. It's easier with people who know what to expect.'

'I know, you said.'

'Can't keep away from you though, can I?'

'Can't you?'

'I probably could, if I had to. I just don't want to.'

'Good.'

'You're different this morning.'

It's true, I am. Something about being away with him like this makes me feel free in a way that I never do when we're back home. I feel a bit more confident somehow, a bit more secure, maybe it's just because I know we're here for the week – it doesn't matter so much if I make a tiny mistake, or say something a bit reckless, because there'll be time to make up for it later.

'I'm just… happy, I guess.'

I turn and smile up at him, I can't help it. He

shakes his head, grinning. I love it when he grins – I've never seen him do it in any of his films. He tugs off his beanie, tousling his hair with his hand at the same time, but then seems to remember himself, and pulls it straight back on again.

'Good. I'm happy too.'

We carry on walking in silence, holding hands, and I try to capture every detail around me in my mind, just like a series of freeze-framed photos. I want to create enough connections in my brain to keep this memory alive for as long as I am.

Later I ask if I can take his photo for real. He's playing around with the fire again, poking about with logs and driftwood and kindling, trying to create the perfect arrangement. I would like to sift through his thoughts, to understand what would make it just right for him, the fire. There's a line of driftwood snaking along the hearth, pieces that he has selected from our walk earlier. I'm shy when I ask him. I won't be surprised if he says no, but I'm worried he'll be annoyed I've asked.

'Aren't there enough pictures of me in the world already?' he asks, gently.

I knew he would say something like this, and I am ready with my answer. I will be brave.

'There are,' I say. 'But they don't come with a memory, do they?'

'What about your film? The installation?'

'It's not the same. I wasn't with you.'

'Maybe not physically, no, but you were in my head.'

'It's just one picture,' I say. 'And then I'll never ask again. You can say no if you want to, but you said last week I never ask you to do anything. So, I'm asking you now. I want something to remember you by.'

'I'm not going anywhere,' but he smiles as he says it, and I know then that he won't refuse me. 'Where do you want me then?'

'Right there. Just carry on with what you're doing. It's not a photoshoot. It just wouldn't have been right to take it without asking is all.'

He goes back to the fire, and I pick up my camera from the coffee table. I fiddle around with the set-tings – it's only a compact, not one I would ever use for work, but I know I will probably only get one shot at this. I want to take it as quickly as possible, so that he does not have time to rearrange his fea-tures in preparation.

'Now,' I say, and he turns to face me.

The wood burner door is still open, and a small cluster of sparks fly out just as I capture the frame. It take us both by surprise, and any tension there might have been over the photo evaporates as they crackle away into the air. Much later, when I develop the image, I will see that the crackles map to the auburn in his hair perfectly, so it is almost as if they have chosen to settle there, but they seem bigger in the photo than they did in reality, and the closeness of the colours seems to create a strange effect where it is not clear if the sparks originate from the fire or from him. His eyes, sparked with embers, will always seem alive to me in that photo in a way in which they have never done in all the pictures I have seen of him before or since. Perhaps I only imagine it, but I seem to see something of my own happiness reflected back in them, that tiny little glint of extraordinary that I have only ever really known with him.

One evening we go to a pub. It's such an ordinary thing to do, just to go to a pub, but this is not like any sort of pub I would ever usually go in. We drive out to Cardigan Bay and, on the way back, we pass through a tiny village with an impossibly difficult name to pronounce. James attempts it, and his Welsh accent makes me smile, but even he can't quite seem to master it.

'There was a pub there,' he says. 'It looked tiny, like it was part of someone's house.'

'Maybe it was.'

'Shall we go back? I remember going somewhere like that when I was a kid, with my mum and dad and Lily.'

'Ok,' I say. 'If you're sure.'

I pull into a layby and turn the car around. I'm finding I enjoy driving on these narrow winding roads more than I thought I would. I've never really driven much on holiday with Dan and the boys. But then, this is not like any holiday I've ever been on with Dan and the boys. I can't remember ever being like this with Dan, even when we first met. Perhaps I'm not being fair though; memory is nothing if not convenient.

The pub is tiny – there's the bar area and the entrance in one half, and then just two benches running down either side in the other. I feel like it's a mistake as soon as we walk in, there is no way in the world we can avoid interaction in here. The woman behind the bar is about the same age as me, a year or two older maybe. To her credit, if she does recognise James, she hides it really well, and we sit down with our drinks at one of the two benches – the one opposite already being occupied by an older couple. They're about the same age as my parents, and clearly already a few drinks in.

'Out without the kiddies are you?' the man asks us. 'I remember those days.'

At first I think it's strange that he would think we'd have kids together, given our age gap, but then it occurs to me almost for the first time that James is of course old enough to have children – it's just

114

that he doesn't. I'd already had both Max and Josh by the time I was his age.

'We're not – ' I begin, but James cuts me off.

'Yeah, just us, date night.'

He says 'date night' like it's in inverted commas, as if he's just some ordinary bloke humouring the wife, and the man laughs. The woman smiles at me conspiratorially, and raises her eyebrows.

'Fancy another?' the man asks us. 'You've got some catching up to do.'

'Sure,' James replies. 'Why not? We'll get the next one.'

He must see the look of panic cross my face.

'I'll drive,' he smiles. 'It is date night.'

I realise I don't know if he even has a licence. It has never occurred to me to ask him before now. I desperately try to remember if I've read anything about him being able to drive online but, in my panic, the information eludes me, if I ever knew it in the first place.

'We're walking,' says the woman, glancing over her shoulder to where the man is now fetching drinks from the bar. 'Thank goodness.'

We chat to them over a couple of rounds. They tell us their names are Elaine and Novello. I confirm to them both that I've indeed never met anyone called Novello before, and Novello himself seems proud of it. We tell them our real names. There seems no reason not to, since they obviously don't have a clue who James is. I can't believe we're really doing this, but I go along with it for James's sake, as he seems to be really enjoying it for some reason.

'Up from London for a few days are you? Kiddies with the grandparents?'

I nod and let James answer for us, and hope they don't ask too many more questions. I needn't worry – he's gone into full blown method acting mode, and they start to tell us how they'd usually be the ones doing the babysitting for their own grandkids themselves. After that, they don't need much more encouragement to tell us all about them and, before we know it, we're scrolling through endless grandchild photos and video footage on Elaine's phone.

As we leave the pub a couple of hours later, I turn back at the door to say thanks to the woman behind the bar.

'You're very welcome,' she replies, smiling knowingly, and tips me a wink as she does so.

I realise then that that, of course, she has realised who James was all along and I wonder if she will tell the other two when we're gone. It actually makes me smile at the thought, and I mouth another, silent, 'thank you' to her as I step out into the now dark sky.

I'm still smiling when I get into the passenger seat of the car. I almost forget and get into the driving seat instead.

'You're not drunk, are you?' James asks.

'Why? You can actually drive, can't you?'

'Of course, I've driven in loads of films.'

'I don't think that's quite the same as driving on real roads though, is it?'

'Well, you'll just have to trust me then, won't you?'

His driving is fine. It's nice just to be able to look at him for a bit, and I curve my body into the window to make it easier. He's still wearing his beanie from when we left the pub and, when he catches me watching him, he laughs and pulls it off, throwing it onto the dashboard, and running his hand through his hair. He must know what he's doing, I think, he must know the effect he has on me, on everyone around him – but I will not look away this time. His hands on the steering wheel and the gears are smooth and delicate, soft, like a girl's. They tell the story of a life without physical work, without domestic work, whatever he might pretend in a pub. They are a blank canvass onto which any life could still be projected. There are lines on his face that weren't there even just a few years ago, but they have done nothing to lessen the overall impact of him. Soften it perhaps, but not lessen it. If anything, he looks even better than he did a decade ago, more realised somehow. He is most definitely a man now though, with just the very first hint of the ruggedness of age yet to creep in. It's too dark to see his eyes properly, but his cheekbones and jawline are even more defined in this light – the stark outline of a mountain range silhouetted against the night sky – tempered only by the faint rash of stubble he has allowed to set in this last day or so. I feel a knot in my chest, and a deepening, just watching him. If I allowed myself to watch him like this more often, I'm not entirely sure I could bear it. The closer you get to a fall, the harder it is to hold back. I tell myself that I am like a teenager around him, but I am not. I am like a teenager around him in one respect only, in that I do not have an adult vocabulary to describe what is happening to me. But I have never felt so adult as an adult before, I have never desired anything, wanted anything, so much. It is like a darkness in me, something so close to abandon that, if I let it go, I will have no control over it at all. It is obsession, yes, but worse than that, compulsion. I have never suffered from addiction, and I cannot help but wonder if this is what it feels like – to want something so much and yet, at the same time, to be terrified of it; to be terrified of both how it makes you feel, and the absence of how it makes you feel.

'So, how did it feel, being married but not married to me?'

'It felt like being married but not married to someone who wasn't you – it was just a character.'

'You didn't like him then?'

'I didn't not like him. He was just someone I met in a pub.'

'It was me underneath though, wasn't it?'

I sigh. 'It's always you underneath, James.'

It is – it's why I fall in love with him in every new role he plays, because I can see him underneath. No matter how well he acts, I can still see him underneath, even when he's playing a bastard. Especially then.

'So, how did it feel?'

I could lie. I don't lie.

'It felt real, but not real. Like a zircon – it looks like a diamond, but it's not. It felt like it would feel real until I knew that it wasn't, and then it wouldn't stop me from liking it, but I would never see it again in the same way. But I did like it though. I can't deny it.'

'A zircon is still real, Kate – it's just not a diamond. If we pretend it's something different, then that's on us. It's not the poor zircon's fault, is it?'

And then it's so ridiculous that we both laugh at

once. I feel like a complete idiot but better that than how I was feeling a minute ago. We sit in silence for a bit, until he interrupts my thoughts again.

'I liked it too. I can't deny it either. I liked it a lot.'

'It was fun, right?'

'It was fun. That's not why I liked it though.'

He is lying horizontally across the bed, with his head resting on my stomach. Even though we are both fully clothed, it still feels almost indecently intimate. It is not yet dusk outside, but the afternoon is fading fast. We haven't bothered to draw the curtains, and the receding light is making me feel sleepy. I know that I should move before I drift off, but I don't want to be the one to break away. My hand drifts to his hair. I love the texture of it; thick and silken. I'd always thought before that he must use some kind of product, but now I know that he doesn't. Today it is stiffened though, sticky with salt and wind, and is leading my thoughts to places I will never likely go. I wonder what it would feel like wet from the sea, gritty with sand. I allow my hand to run all the way through to the ends, rubbing them between my fingertips, and then return to the roots again, massaging his scalp. He sighs, almost a moan, brushing his face against me, pushing deeper.

'Did you see your family at Christmas?' I ask.

It's clumsy, and I regret it instantly. Stroking his hair like this, there is something almost maternal about it, and yet there isn't.

He laughs, burrowing deeper still. His voice is muffled.

'You think I'm trying to get into your womb?'

'No, not that. Well, maybe that a bit. Maybe you do see me as some kind of mother figure, you know, like a sugar daddy.'

'My mum's fine, Kate, I don't need another one. And anyway, I told you, you're not old enough for that.'

'I know, I'm not trying to analyse you. Well, maybe I am a bit. I just can't work you out, I can't work this out.'

'I am, you know – trying to get into your womb. Not in the way you think though.'

I don't really know what he means, so I wait. I don't want to say something else I'll regret. This is no longer the lazy, horizontal conversation of just a moment ago, and we are both upright now, sharpened by the edge that has crept in.

'We could have a baby.'

It's my turn to laugh, but I do not quite manage the light-hearted tone I am aiming for, and it comes out as something more like a sneer.

'I'm too old.'

'No you're not, loads of women your age do. It's not unusual at all these days.'

'It's still risky. And I am too old – I feel too old.'

'We'd find a good doctor obviously.'

I laugh again, somewhat nervously. 'It's not going to happen.'

'Or we could adopt.'

'We're not going to adopt. We don't even live together. We're not even a couple.'

'Don't you think I'd be a good dad?'

'Yes, of course you would. You will. Just not with me.'

'Why not? We could get married.'

I sigh. 'Sure, let's get married, let's live happily ever after, let's have a kid. What could possibly go wrong?'

'I'm not playing. Why couldn't we get married? Why shouldn't we be together like that? What's stopping us?'

'Oh, only the age difference, and the fact that you're 'you', and I'm married, and I already have kids, and it's only a matter of time before you break my heart anyway. Only that you might have broken it already. Only that.'

'You're being ridiculous.'

'I'm being ridiculous?'

'Yes, this age thing, it's stupid. So there's, what, ten years between us right?'

'Eleven.'

'So what? There's nine years between my mum and dad. How old is your husband? Christ, half the guys I work with have wives half their age. Who cares about any of that these days? If anyone ever did?'

'I care. Everyone else would care. You know it's different for a woman. Everyone would just be waiting for you to find someone younger, someone more like you. I'd be waiting for that. I'd be looking for it. All this, whatever this is, whatever it is we have. It would kill it. You know that. I don't even think you see me that way anyway.'

'I thought you weren't trying to analyse me?' He says this through gritted teeth, and I realise I have never felt him angry before. 'You think I'd get into something like this lightly? You think this is easy for me? You don't know me at all if that's what you think.'

'You're right, I don't know you, and you don't know me. I'm just a normal person, ordinary. And you're not – this isn't. I don't want to see myself all over tomorrow's papers. I've got my kids – my actual, real-life kids – to think about.'

He looks like he's been physically slapped in the face. I can't believe I have done it to him. I ought to feel terrible, but I don't, not at all. I feel angry too. He's acting like a child, I think, a child who has never been denied anything. And I am like a toy that he will demand in the supermarket, but will be forgotten in a day.

'So, what you're saying is I'm not worth it?'

'No, I'm not saying that – I'm saying the risk is too high.'

'That's bullshit. And it's just another way of saying the same thing anyway. It wouldn't be too high if you loved me.'

'I don't love you, because it's not real. This isn't real, none of it is. It's not your world or mine. I can't exist, I can't be, in your life, in your real life, and you can't be in mine. That's why you've been keeping me secret, isn't it?'

'You're wrong. I've been keeping this secret precisely because it is real, to me, and because I keep everything real secret. But I can't keep it secret forever. I can't protect you forever.'

'I know that. It's you who's confused – not me.'

'Confused? Yeah, right, that's it, of course, confused.'

He doesn't slam the door on the way out, but closes it quietly and gently behind him.

He sleeps on the sofa that night. At first I think he might leave completely and, for a time, I almost want him to. I never did draw the curtains and, just as the sky at last begins to lighten outside, unable to bear it any longer, I go in to him. He is sleeping with the psychedelic throw pulled up under his chin, and I feel a slight pang of guilt for not even fetching him a proper blanket from where I know there are some stowed at the top of the wardrobe. I sit down on the floor with my back against the sofa at first, reluctant to disturb him. We will be going home today and, if this is the end, I don't want it to be like this. Eventually, I shake him gently to wake him up. He doesn't say anything at first, just opens the blanket up for me to lie down beside him. Then he covers us both up again, tucking us in together, nose to nose, and something in me shifts, lurches. It's not that I haven't felt protective of him before – I have. Even before I knew him, I had. But this is something else. This feeling is more like responsibility than protectiveness and, even though it fits, I don't like the shape of it.

'I'm sorry,' I say. 'I do love you. Even though I know it's ridiculous, I can't help it.'

'I'm sorry too.' He catches my hand, fingertips to fingertips. 'I can't help it either.'

We take one last walk on the beach before we go. It's still early, and we have even beaten the dog walkers. I somehow seem to be a lot further away from home than I did at the beginning of the week, and the journey back seems almost daunting. I feel lightheaded, and something almost like seasickness. Like the feeling you get on a rollercoaster, just before it plummets. He stops, pulls me gently towards him. I am already crying.

'Kate...' he says, and I imagine in that moment he will ask if he can kiss me, and I do not want him to ask, more than anything I do not want him to ask.

And then his lips are on mine anyway, with only the lightest of touches at first, just as we have kissed so many times before. Only this time I part my lips, slightly, hesitantly, but nonetheless unequivocally. I want to give this, if only this. I want to take this, if only this. It is the most exquisitely delicate kiss I could ever have imagined and yet it is also the most passionate, fluttering in its intensity. And then I am out of control, just as I have always feared I would be. My hands are in his hair and I don't know if I am pulling him to the ground, to the still wet sand, or if he is pulling me. We are a bundle of coats, and hands, and mouths, and mess. I have never wanted anyone or anything like this, it is as if nothing else matters. There is only this moment; there is only this. My hands are under his coat, now pulling at his clothes. The empty beach is outside of my field of awareness – it is not that I don't care who sees, I don't even think of it. I lose all sense of where I am. It feels timeless, primal, brutal. And then he is pulling away, gently at first, but now firmer.

'Kate… Kate… stop, we need to stop.'

Now I'm confused. It doesn't quite register. Didn't he kiss me first? Doesn't he want me now that he has me? I don't want to stop. I know that he's saying no but I don't want to hear it. I keep on anyway. He is holding my hands, but he is pulling still further away from me, keeping me at arm's length.

'You have to stop, Kate. You have to stop now, or I won't be able to.'

And I do stop then. God, I feel so ashamed, so disgusted at myself. I pull my hands away from him, draw my knees up to my chest, burying my face in them. Hot tears soaking into my jeans. The warmth is almost scalding.

'I'm sorry,' I choke. 'I can't believe I just did that. I hate myself.'

I don't want to look at him. I don't see how he will ever forgive me when I know that I will never forgive myself. There is no way back from this. He tries to put his arm around me, and I shrug him off.

'No, Kate, I'm sorry. What? You think I don't want you? Is that it?' His voice is shaking. 'I just need you to be sure you want this, is all. I mean, really want this. I need to be sure you want this. It's like I told you before, right at the beginning, in Kent, remember? I don't want to fuck this up. I feel like I already did, last night. I love you, alright? I know it's fucked up, I know it's too soon, but there's no point me trying to hide it now, is there? I mean,

I've practically asked you to marry me already, haven't I?'

And I laugh in spite of myself. I can't help it.

So, we put the key back in the tin, and we leave Saundersfoot behind us, and we hardly speak at all for the rest of the day. Like an old couple who have run out of things to say to one another. It is almost like being with Dan. It is almost a relief.

ELEVEN

He is different tonight, edgy. Everything between us has changed since Pembrokeshire, just as I knew it would. He's getting bored of me, I think, of this, I knew it would happen.

'Why don't we go out?' he asks, as if it was the most natural thing in the world, and I laugh.

'We don't have to do this,' I say.

'No, I mean it. Why don't we just go out?'

'You know why.'

'No, I don't. Why shouldn't we go out if we want to? We could watch a film, you know, in an actual cinema – Tom Hardy has a new one.'

He smiles, but it feels a bit dangerous somehow, and I remember I don't know him at all. He wouldn't hurt me physically, I know that, but he could still destroy every other part of me. And I don't know him well enough to know he won't do that – not really.

'Or we could just go to a restaurant. You know, like normal people do. You're a normal person, aren't you? What would you do if you were here with your husband?'

We have still not spoken about Dan explicitly, and it takes me off guard.

'What would you do if you were here with your girlfriend?' I snap back. 'Hold a press conference?'

We have never spoken about Saskia Hamilton before either. Before I'd met him, I'd read all about their relationship, of course, but I didn't really enjoy it much – not even then. I realise I have not checked any of my social media accounts for three months, just to avoid seeing him with her, or with anyone, or doing any of the things he does when we're not together.

And I feel such a rage surge up in me then that I realise I don't even know myself that well as it turns out either. Tears prick my eyes, and I turn away to the window, my forehead pressed against the cool of the glass. I see the lights of Holborn trailing away towards the west end and I can't help but wonder if it would be so bad to go out after all. Maybe it's better to just get it over with. This thing, whatever it is, this bubble of escape for both of us, it surely couldn't survive the outside world, could it? And there would be a sweetness in knowing everything it had been and everything it had never been, in just knowing, like the certainty of death, a relief in the end that it is done and over with. And it will feel like a death when it comes. I know that.

'Are you jealous?' he asks. 'Of Saskia?'

He is teasing me, and his tone is amused, but it's too considered. He's acting. There's something underneath. Excitement? Relief? Satisfaction?

'Don't do that.' I say, but the words collect like stones in my mouth.

He comes up behind me then. I can hardly bear it, knowing that this might be the last time I will feel him near me like this. His hands settle on my shoulders, thumbs resting either side of my vertebrae. I anticipate the kiss on the back of my neck before I feel it, the softest, almost imperceptible brush of his lips. Perhaps I only imagine it. I hold myself rigid to try and contain the shiver inside, but he must know, of course he knows.

'I'm sorry,' he says. 'I am, honestly. This really isn't how I wanted tonight to go. I have to tell you something, and I didn't want it to be in a hotel room, is all. Please can we just go out somewhere? Just for a drink or something, I promise.'

His own words are thick and deceptive in their sweetness, and I choke back a sob.

'Hey,' he breathes, turning me round to face him, kissing the top of my head. 'Come on, it'll be fine. I've brought my disguise.'

He nods to the hoody slung over the chair by the desk, and I can't help but laugh. Everything is just the same as it has always been.

We find an Italian in a cobbled alleyway, just off the High Road. There's another couple and a work party. The waitress tells us we can take our pick and we opt for a table in the corner at the back. The lighting's subdued and I start to think it might not be so bad after all, we might be able to survive this night after all. It's not until the waitress comes back with our drinks order that she realises it's James. I smile at her in what I hope is a reassuring manner and, thankfully, she doesn't say anything. James still doesn't make eye contact with her, but perhaps it's easier for him this way, and he's had longer to get used to it I suppose. We eat olives and table bread, and he asks me about what I'm going to work on next and I tell him about the new exhibition and it feels so good to actually talk to someone about it, that I'm able to let go and just allow myself to show my enthusiasm for once.

'Kate,' he says, and I remember he'd said there was something he wanted to talk to me about. 'I'm working away for a few months, in Paris.'

Oh, Paris. 'How lovely. When do you go?'

'Tomorrow. I've been meaning to tell you, I should have told you, I know – I didn't think it was going to be quite so soon. But anyway, they're ready to start now so there it is. It shouldn't be too long, four months tops.'

I don't know what to say. I knew this was coming,

of course I did. This is his job. I realise he's hardly even mentioned it since we met.

'Kate?'

He takes my hand, and traces a circle in my palm.

'I've got something for you, I mean I've got something I want you to have. It's a bit weird, so I don't know whether to tell you or just give it to you. I don't want you to get freaked out.'

He glances over his shoulder, quickly, and pulls something out from the pocket of his hoody – a box, a ring box. He slides it across the table.

'It's an engagement ring.'

I open the box. It is the most exquisite piece of jewellery I have ever seen in my life.

'It's an engagement ring, but it's not an engagement ring. I'm not asking you to marry me or anything – not really. I know you've already done that, and you have kids, and I know you don't want it. It's just, I've never wanted to buy anyone an engagement ring before, never even thought of it before, but I really wanted to get one for you. I can't explain it, I know it doesn't make any kind of sense, but does any of it?'

'James, I – '

'Just think of it as an engagement ring, but not an engagement ring, if it helps. You know, like wait, but don't wait.'

There is a pause – a moment, I suppose, of something like possibility, or a suspension of the inevitable at least. Then the door, swept open by a breeze from somewhere, a flurry of flashes, another pause, James's this time, and he does the strangest thing – he holds up his hands in the air as if to say 'you've got me' and smiles in the direction of the photographer in the open doorway. It is over almost as soon as it begins, and the waitress is shooing the photographer away again, pushing him out in a cloud of steam and heat.

'We're closed,' she says, slamming and bolting the door behind him.

'I'm so sorry,' she says, crossing back towards us. 'I didn't call them, I promise. You can go out through the kitchen if you want.'

She catches sight of the ring on the table. I ought to have snapped the box shut tight. I hope it doesn't show up in the photo.

'Oh Christ,' she says. 'It's beautiful.'

'It's not what you think,' I say.

'Oh, I think it is, lucky lady,' and she smiles at James.

For the first time, he does make eye contact with her, and smiles right back. He's not acting, he seems genuinely happy.

'Oh, my heart!' she says, comically clutching her chest. 'Go on, get out quick, before he finds his way round the back.'

We run back to the hotel, laughing manically, holding hands all the way. I don't think I can remember the last time I laughed so hard. I'm not sure I ever have. By the time we get back to the suite, I'm gasping for breath and, suddenly serious, James asks me to try it on – the ring. It fits perfectly.

'How did you…?'

He makes a shape with his fingers, and shrugs. And I laugh. And it should be a joyous moment. In any other lifetime, it would be a joyous moment. A pinprick of light shining like a beacon through the years to come. But this is not that life, and my life is not that life. I am not that person. So, instead, a kind of coolness creeps up on me, and I cannot help but think of Dan, about how he would never be able to remember the shape of me, about how he would not even try to, and it is a pain that I do not deserve to feel, so I separate myself from it. And then I remember, this is our last time together, of course it is. He will be gone in the morning, to Paris, and I will never see him again. It all makes sense now, the ring is goodbye, even if he does not yet know it himself. I will never have this night returned to me – it can only be lived now – and, for once, I am glad of that eleven-year age gap between us. I am old enough to recognise this moment for what it is, and to face it unflinchingly, with agency. I no longer have the possibility of what might still remain. Everything has been leading to this point, and this point is the end of everything. Not a gradual entropy, but a singularity. It was never about this; it was always about this. It is only a step to narrow the space between us, and I look up to meet his gaze, as his lowers to meet mine. His eyes, not blue or green as I used to imagine, but grey, and bound to me now. My hand lifts, almost involuntarily, to the side of his face. I trace his jawline, slightly roughened from the day that has passed. He sighs, and I wait. I wait. I wait. The kiss when it comes is not fluttery and light-headed like in Pembrokeshire, but resolute, determined, with the certainty of death.

'Kate, Kate…'

He's gently shaking me awake. I smile up at him and, for a moment, I forget that I'm looking up at the most beautiful man in the world and pull his face back down towards mine. Perhaps it is only a dream anyway.

'Oh, god, Kate, I wish I could stay but I can't. I need to get to the airport, I've left it as late as I can.'

Oh, yes, Paris. It is not a dream. I swallow down the tears that are already forming.

'Look, last night, they'll be stuff in the papers today, when I'm gone. They'll find you Kate.'

I blink and rub my eyes.

'What are you saying? That I mustn't talk to the papers? Do you think I would?'

'No, it's not that. I mean your husband, your kids. I don't know what you've told them about us.'

'Us?'

'Yes, Kate, us. It's going to be hard for you, I know, and I'm not going to be here for you. But I will be here, you can ring me – you know that, right? You never ring me.'

'Here, but not here.'

'Yes, here, but not here. But really here. I don't know how long it'll take you to sort everything out. I mean, obviously don't worry about the money or anything. You don't need money, do you? I'll get Julie to sort you out an account.'

I don't understand. Money? What, is he trying to buy me off or something? None of this makes any sense.

'Money?'

'Yes, just let him have everything. Try and get it all done as smoothly as possible. I mean, if he wants money, that's fine. Just get everything sorted here and then come to Paris. Take as long as you need, only not too long – I'm not sure I'm going to be able to work. I'll be waiting.'

'Waiting, but not waiting?'

'No, Kate. Really fucking waiting – as in, every fucking minute I'll be waiting. God, just promise me you won't falter when I'm gone. Promise me.'

I still don't get it.

'I don't understand what you want me to do. You want me to get money from Julie to pay that photographer off?'

'The photographer? What are you talking about? I'm saying you might need money for your husband. You might need to rent somewhere. I mean, don't rent somewhere – come to Paris. But you might need to put stuff in storage. And they'll be solicitors. It might not seem like it now, but these things escalate quickly, don't they?'

'You think Dan's going to throw me out when he sees that photo?'

'No, it's not about the photo, Kate, it's about us.'

'Us?'

'Yes, us, for fuck's sake. How many times do I need to say it? Look, I really need to go. God, I hate myself right now. But you're not making this any easier, are you?'

'Are you saying you want us to be together? Like, properly together? You want me to divorce Dan?'

'Yes, of course. Don't you? And you don't have to divorce him, if you don't want to. I don't care about that. Just tell him you're leaving, obviously make sure your kids as ok as they can be, and come to Paris. We can sort out the details later.'

'The details? You think my whole life is 'details'?'

'No, of course not – only that there'll be stuff to sort out, and we don't have to do everything all at once. You don't have to do everything all at once. I can help you. I thought… I don't know what I thought. After last night… I mean I thought that was that. I thought you'd decided, that you'd decided on me – on us. No, not that, that's not what I mean. I know your kids are more important, obviously. But they're teenagers, aren't they? You're not going to stay with your husband for the sake of your kids surely? I thought, after last night, now that we were finally together, you know, properly, we were finally together – properly. For real. I don't get it. If that's not what this is, what is it then?'

Something has shifted in his tone.

'I thought it was goodbye. I didn't think I would ever see you again.'

He looks just for a moment as if he might cry, but then he's up, pulling on clothes, shoving stuff into a holdall. And, almost as soon as it starts, the panic in me is too big, all encompassing. This is not the feeling of melancholic resignation I had anticipated. It is the biggest fear I have ever experienced. Existential.

'Please, James, you can't go now, not like this. It has been real, hasn't it? What we've felt? You know it has.'

I sound desperate, I know, but I can't control it. The words are not mine. They come from a place inside I have never been to.

'Please, don't ruin it, it's all I'll have. When you're gone, it's all I'll have. I need to know. I need to know it was real. Whatever it was, I need to know.'

I can't breathe, the tears are lodged in my throat, choking me – I can no longer swallow them down, but I can't let them out either.

'Unbelievable. Just unbelievable.'

He is spitting the words out now.

'So, last night, last night was – what? A one-night stand for you? Friends with benefits? Jesus. Talk about not reading the room. I knew you'd had doubts. But I thought, I thought... I thought you'd made up your mind, like I had. Why the hell did you even agree to go out with me last night if you thought it was over? You must have known what would happen.'

'You're not being fair – you know I didn't want to go. I was worried someone would recognise you, you know that.'

'Of course they would. We were in the middle of London, for Christ's sake. You must have known how I felt, what I was thinking. You think I haven't learnt by now never to be seen with someone unless it's serious?'

'You make it sound like you planned it.'

There is an edge to my own voice now, under the tears. I can't help it, I feel manipulated.

'I didn't set it up, if that's what you mean. But I knew it would happen, of course I did.'

'So I was right not to trust you then.'

'You were right not to trust me? You were right not to trust me? You've been playing me, this whole time. Is that all this was? All I was? Just a bit of fun, and then back to your husband?'

'No, you know that's not true. I've never felt this way about anyone. Never about Dan. But it was always going to end like this, wasn't it? Or it would've just fizzled out, once you'd had enough of me. It was always going to end somehow.'

'I can't believe how wrong I got it. All this time, all this time, I thought we were at the start of something, and you thought we were at the end. How did you think I was going to feel?'

'I – I didn't think about it. I was only thinking about how I was going to feel.'

The finality of my own words slam into me, and even I can't quite believe how bad they sound. And I realise it sounds bad because it is bad. What did I think he was? Indestructible? All this time, I'd been wanting to get to know the real person. Hadn't I told him not to act with me? Made him promise not to? But I'd tried so hard to exclude the outside world from these moments of perfection together, it was almost as if he didn't exist, couldn't exist, beyond that. I'd objectified him in the worst way possible, and he couldn't hate me more than I hated myself. If I'd felt unworthy, it was because I was unworthy – not because I wasn't young enough, or beautiful enough, or exceptional enough, but because I couldn't see that he was more than all of those things. And I need to tell him, I need to tell him now, that I am sorry, before he goes, but the words won't come, they are lodged in my chest, obstructing my breathing, and I cannot cough them up. He is at the door now, and the tears finally crack his voice.

'Well, you'll have plenty of time to think about it now, won't you? While you enjoy the rest of your normal fucking no risk life.'

And then he's gone, really gone, and I'm retching, gasping for breath, the air unable to reach my lungs, drowning under the weight of a responsibility that ought not fit, and I don't get out of that bed again until they come to change it.

TWELVE

On the way back I text him. Long rambling incoherent letters of texts. I even try to call, but I can't get through. After a while, I realise he's blocked me, but still I think he'll calm down. It's over, I know that, but I can't believe he will let it end like this. I trust him not to let it end like this. Even on this short journey, I find myself forgetting, still expecting a text or to hear his voice at any moment. I didn't realise how dependent I have become on those flashes of light throughout the day after all, and the anticipation between them, even when we're apart, especially when we're apart. I wonder how long it will take to not forget that he's gone. In this moment, it seems like I will never quite remember – like a smoker who still thinks to themselves it's time for a cigarette even though they quit two decades ago.

I am not expecting anyone to be home. The boys must have left for school, but Dan's car is in the drive. I'm not ready for this yet. I might even end up telling him, I think. I don't want to, but it's so close to the surface, I can't be sure it won't come out. In fact, I'm sure it will come out. If he is kind to me, it will be worse.

He is not kind to me, and it is still worse. Even as I turn the key in the lock, the air feels charged with something. I know instantly, I can feel it like a sudden chill, he has been waiting for me. I feel dirty. I should have had a shower before I left the hotel. I could have done. I could have gone back to my own room and not checked out 'til lunchtime.

'Where have you been?'

The question catches me off guard. It has been weeks since he has asked me.

'Why?'

His tone is coldly casual. 'Oh, you know, no real reason, I just thought you might tell me the truth for a change.'

'I've been in town.'

'Been in town for what?'

'I don't want to talk about it. Not now. I know we need to, but you've been putting it off too. You know that.'

I turn to leave the room, but he grabs my arm and pulls me back. I'm shocked, he's never done anything like that in twenty years of marriage. Strange that he should now, when it's over anyway, when it has been for years. I ought to be angry, furious even, but it is as if my capacity to feel anything other than complete devastation this morning has become muted somehow. It is then that I notice the newspaper on the dining room table, not one that either of us would ever buy – a tabloid. I realise now that his gaze has been falling back to it the whole time I've been home, it's why my eye has been drawn to it too.

'Don't you want to see it then? Your picture in the paper – with your boyfriend.'

He opens the paper to a few pages in. It's not on the front cover at least. Of course, it isn't. It's only celebrity gossip after all. But the headline is huge and, along with the photo, the piece takes up a whole page.

'Mamma Mia! James Talisker spotted in secret Italian tryst with chubby housewife.'

I feel sick – there is nothing even about the installation, about how we met. They must know who I am, as they have mentioned me by name further down, but they've obviously not allowed themselves to be constrained by detail.

'It's not what you think.'

'Well, that depends, doesn't it? On what you think I think. They rang me at work, Kate, to ask me for a comment. A comment, for fuck's sake.'

'Have you been in then?'

'Yes, of course I've been in, but then I came home

again obviously. I had to google both your names to find out what the hell you've been up to. And I still don't know.'

'You know about the installation then?'

'I do now – and the others. It doesn't explain why you're still seeing him though, does it? Although I suppose it explains why you've been in town so much lately. Am I supposed to just be ok with it? Like that hall pass thing – except you've gone and done it for real.'

'I told you, it's not like that.'

'Oh, for fuck's sake, I know it's not like that. He's a fucking film star who, according to Google, lives with a supermodel for Christ's sake. Apparently they're supposed to be getting engaged any day now. Obviously he's not going to be interested in you, is he?'

He might as well have hit me.

'Well, if you're so sure about that, then what is your problem exactly?'

'My problem is I would rather you'd been having an affair with some normal bloke down the road – it's what I thought you were doing anyway. This is just pathetic – it makes you look pathetic, and it makes us look pathetic too. How do you think the boys are going to feel when they find out?'

'You would rather I was having an affair with one of our neighbours than having an exhibition in a major London gallery? Can you even hear your-self? And maybe the boys might be, you know, just a tiny bit proud when they find out. Perhaps I might have even told you if you'd been the slight-est bit interested in my work.'

'I am interested in your work – your actual work. As a matter of fact, I'd really like to know when you're going to get back to it.'

'You know what? It's none of your business. It's no longer your concern.'

'You're not having the house.'

'I don't want it. I'm going to my parents.'

'Good. I'd have a shower first if I were you though. You look like a fucking mess.'

I do have a shower, and then I pack a bag and load it into the car. I will have to come back, of course, but I have what I need for now. And then I sit down in the lounge and wait for the boys to get home from school. I can't cry, not yet. I need to hold it together until I can get out of here. I am in suspended animation – I know that the crash is coming, this is just the freeze frame in between. I try and work through the practicalities in my mind, but I keep missing a step and then having to go back to the beginning again. I try to not let the idea that James expected me to be thinking about practicalities today creep in. Everything is as he expected it to be, and as I expected it to be, and yet none of it is as either of us expected. I can't think about it yet, I can't allow myself to, but it seems like such a cruel punishment to be doing the very thing I would have been doing anyway if things had been different. If I had been different. I'll say sorry, I think, and then I try to push it to one side again. I'll say sorry and then things will go back to normal, our normal. I'll have time. I know it can't last forever, I know that, but I'll have time to prepare myself for it. It won't be like this, it will be different. I will be different.

So, I think about the practicalities. I will go to Mum and Dad's. I will give the boys the option to come too but, of course, they won't want to. It will be better if they don't really, it will give me time to sort things out. I'll get a flat, with a room for each of them, so they can come whenever they want. Max won't – what would be the point now? Maybe he'll stay with me in the holidays sometimes. Josh might. He'll stay with Dan for a bit but he'll come to me eventually. But how will I see James? When Josh is with Dan I suppose. It will be ok with Dan. Once he realises I really am letting him have the house, he'll want to keep things civil. He'll be mistrustful at first but he'll be ok after a while. I'll have to be careful. I need to ring my agent, to see what I've got coming in, but it'll be enough for a deposit – maybe even for a mortgage. And

I'll work, of course I'll work. Not now, not today, but soon. I need to check my diary for weddings. I might need them now. I can get more if I add the installation to my website. I can't think about that now. I can't use him to make money. I could add the Amber Cross one though, and the new one. Chubby housewife. Am I fat? I didn't think so before, maybe I am. Is it better that no one will believe the story or worse? Better that my own husband didn't believe the story or worse?

The boys get back at the same time, chatting about something and laughing as they come through the door. They both go straight to their own rooms. I could call them into the lounge and tell them both at the same time, but I decide to go into them separately instead. It's better that way, more normal.

I go into Max first. There's no easy way to say it, so I just say it.

'I need to tell you something. Me and Dad are splitting up. I'm going to Grandma's. You can come too if you want, or you can stay here – you're old enough to decide for yourself. I'll get a flat or something, so they'll always be a room for you once I'm settled. You know, when you come back from uni and stuff. I'm sorry, Max.'

I'm trying to keep it monotone, it wouldn't be fair to break down in front of him. You have to be the adult here, I tell myself over and over. He doesn't say anything, just a slight incline of his chin to acknowledge what I've told him, pale faced.

'Are you ok?' I ask.

He nods. 'I'm fine. I was expecting it, I guess.'

'You knew this would happen?'

'I knew it ought to.'

For a moment I think I will ask him what he means but, of course, I know. And then I feel the slow creep of shame at the awareness that my seventeen year old son has seen our situation for what it is, maybe even more clearly than I have seen it myself. I wonder how long he has known for. I have been reckless in my inaction, I think.

Josh tears up when I tell him. I try to hug him, but he pulls away from me.

'You can come to Grandma's with me,' I say, 'if you want to. You can come any time. And I'll get a flat or something – you'll always have your own room with me, even if you stay with Dad.'

'I'll stay here. I don't want to go.'

'It's ok,' I say. 'I know.'

He hates change, I know that, just like Dan. But he will come to me eventually. I know that too.

THIRTEEN

It is dark by the time I leave. I take the extended route home, making the drive last. I have always enjoyed driving familiar routes at night, especially this one. It doesn't feel strange to me that I should still think of Mum and Dad's as home, even after all these years, but it does make me wonder why then I have left it so long to do this – if my own house still wasn't.

Mum offers me my old room, apologising again that it's now a guest room, but I tell her I'll take Zoe's instead. I can feel her energy in here, like the space is alive with her. I swear I can still smell the patchouli and coconut and dewberry of her teenage years, it seems ingrained in the walls somehow even though most of the furnishings have changed. I crawl into my sister's bed, fully clothed, and wait for sleep. When it comes it is fitful and I can't get comfortable. There's a tiredness and a tightness in my chest, but the thoughts won't stop. Even though I know they will, eventually, I don't know that they will eventually. I clutch my phone to my chest, willing it to vibrate. The panic is rising up in me again and there is nowhere to take it. No one to fight with, no one to run to, just a growing realisation that maybe this is it after all. This really is how it ends – in silence and nothingness. I clench my teeth, dig my fingernails into my palms until I think my fingers might break, screw all of my muscles into tight knots, but there is no release for this feeling. No way to push it any further inwards. I have romanticised this separation in the same way that I have romanticised everything else, daydreaming of a calm, considered, unbearably sad acceptance. But that, as it turns out, was no more real than the rest of it and I am left with nothing. I am nothing. It is as if I never existed. I do not even exist to myself except as a conduit for this pain. I cannot separate myself from it. There is only this. I cannot even think about how long it will last because I cannot see beyond it. I am like a wounded animal that must now know it will die but is somehow still alive. And while it is not dead it must hope, a delirium of hope that is somehow worse than the pain itself.

On my second night back, Zoe comes home too. The sound of her key in the lock is unmistakable and I can hear her talking in hushed tones with Mum in the kitchen below. The volume of the TV in the lounge rises slightly, Dad must be keeping out of it. She comes in with a carrier bag, jangling with bottles, and two glasses. She passes me a glass of red and does not say anything until I finish it. When I do, she nods, silently refills it and hands it back to me, then she pours one for herself and sits down on the beanbag in the corner, sipping slowly.

'I have to say, Kate, I'm slightly surprised,' she says, when she speaks at last. 'I mean, I knew this was on the cards, but I genuinely didn't think it would hit you so badly.'

I don't know where to start.

'I've never felt like this before,' I say.

'Ah, I see – before Dan, you mean. No, I suppose I was always the one with the broken hearts, wasn't I? You were always so sensible.'

And then the tears come choking out, and I am losing my breath again. Zoe deftly relieves me of my glass, before I spill it everywhere, and comes to sit next to me on the bed, her arm wrapped awkwardly round my shoulders. We have never been very physical, and I try to push the tears back down again so that she will not feel the need to comfort me like this. It's not helping anyway.

'It's not about Dan,' I say. 'I don't care about Dan.'

'Come on, you've been married for twenty odd years, it's only natural to feel like this.'

'I'm telling you, it's not about Dan. Breaking up with Dan is the only good thing to come out of this. I never should have married him – I see that now.'

'The kids then. I get it – you've never really been away from them properly before, have you?'

'I do miss the boys…' I choke on the words. 'But it's not that.'

I'm going to tell her, I know I'm going to tell her, I just don't yet know how.

'What then?'

'I – I've been seeing someone. No, not like that. I mean, I fell in love, that's all. Like properly in love, like I've never been before. And now it's over. I've just had my heart broken is all.'

'Ah,' she says again. 'Who was it?'

What's the point in lying? She's my sister, and Dan will probably tell Chris anyway.

'James Talisker.'

It doesn't register.

'Where did you meet him?'

'James Talisker, as in James Talisker, the actor.'

She laughs a bit awkwardly. I can see she thinks it's an attempt at humour, a shot at making light of the situation somehow. But, of course, it doesn't work as a joke because it's just not funny. There is no punchline. I wait, deadpan, for it to sink in. And then I know that it does because she stops with the awkward laughing and she's looking at me with evident concern instead.

'What happened?'

I can see what she's worried about, I can almost see the possibilities running behind her eyes. She knows now it's some kind of mental health issue, but she doesn't yet understand the nature of it or the full extent. I decide to put her out of her misery.

'Don't worry, it's not what you're thinking. Well, it is sort of what you're thinking. I mean, I was seeing him – not like seeing him, seeing him. But seeing him, as in actually seeing him, as in we were meeting up, you know, in a planned way, as in he agreed to it – since the Autumn.'

There's a flicker of doubt, of course there is, but then she's my sister and if she doesn't believe me no one will – and I see that she knows this too, she understands it. It might take her a second or two, but she sees in that instant that it is less harmful to believe a lie than to doubt the truth. It is a concession that no one else in this world other than my sister would ever make for me, could ever understand, and it is so characteristic of her to make it that I am almost blindsided by my love for her, by hers for me, even in the midst of all this.

'Jesus Christ, Kate. You don't do things by halves do you.'

She hands me back my wine and I allow her a smile.

'I'll be ok now,' I say, gulping on my wine.

She nods and, taking the hint, takes up her own

place again, back on the beanbag. The print is faded, but I think it must have been a-ha originally – Morten Harket's face long absorbed into the material, as if he has disappeared into the fabric of time itself, I think, as if we all have.

'I'm surprised you didn't take that with you,' I say, nodding towards the beanbag.

'Yeah, I don't think Chris would have appreciated it somehow. You could always use your own room. If you don't like it.'

'I prefer it in here – fits with the teenage angst I suppose.'

I will do this, laugh at myself, it is what is expected. It's what we all do, isn't it? Pretend to be ok when we're not. The stronger the feelings, the easier it is to hide them, the more invested we are in keeping them hidden.

'And Dan… Dan knows?'

'Well, sort of – it's complicated.'

'Of course it is.'

'I mean, he knows some of it. I had an exhibition, you see, and James – well, James was the subject. Dan knows about that, and he knows I've been seeing him. But he doesn't – he doesn't know everything.'

'So you haven't actually been having an affair then?'

I hesitate.

'Not exactly.'

'What does that mean?'

'Not in the normal sense, no.'

'You mean it's not physical – you're in love with him, but it's not physical?'

'Zoe, it's James Talisker...'

'Fair. So, what then? It's unrequited?'

'Yes, I'm in love with him. Yes, it's unrequited. Well, it is now anyway. It was physical, but not physical. I can't really explain it. I've never felt it before. I knew it wasn't going anywhere, of course I did. It's not that – it's just, it's just how it's ended...'

'Did you sleep with him?'

'Only once.'

'I don't mean, did you sleep with him, sleep with him. I mean, did you shag him.'

'I know what you mean.'

'Ok, that's better then.'

'How is that better?'

'You'll get over this, Kate, you know you will. It might not seem like it now, but you will eventually. Just like I did all those times. And, when you do, it will be a memory – and I hope and trust it will be a good fucking memory. But it will be something you've done, rather than something you've not done. And, Jesus Christ Kate, no one's ever gonna beat this as an anecdote, are they?'

'I don't want you to think – he didn't use me for sex. And he didn't feel sorry for me either. It wasn't that. It was something – it was something for him too.'

My voice breaks again on this. There is so much I want to tell her and yet so much I don't, so much I can't.

'And Dan doesn't know?'

I can't help but smile at this.

'No, Dan has been married to me for nearly two decades – he could just about believe I might be shagging one of the neighbours, James Talisker was a step too far.'

'So you could go back if you wanted to?'

'I'm not going back.'

She nods.

'Kate, I wasn't sure whether to tell you this now, but Dan – I think he's been seeing other people too.'

'It's ok, I know.'

'You know?'

'Well, I thought he probably was. How do you know?'

'I only found out yesterday. You know my friend,

Jo? She was there when mum called – I told her you'd split up with Dan, and she said she'd seen him on some apps… I would've told you, obviously, I just didn't know how you'd take it, you know – I didn't want to kick you when you were already down.'

'It's fine. I hope he finds someone – it's better that way.'

'Did you never love him then?'

'I did, of course I did. But just not enough really, when it came down to it. Not like this. I didn't think this was possible – for me, that is. I thought I was being sensible with Dan, realistic, you know – not like…'

'Not like me.'

'I didn't want to say it, but yeah – all those bastards, all those times you had your heart broken black and blue. I didn't get it, why you couldn't just find someone half decent and settle down.'

'The same reason you won't now – now you know what it feels like. And then I met Chris…'

'Exactly, you met Chris, and I realised you could have both. You could settle with someone you really loved after all, and I was so happy for you, I still am. All the time I thought you were the one taking all the risks, but really it was me. I was sticking on Dan, all that time, I was just sticking. And it wasn't fair to him either, was it? I hope he does find someone new now, someone who deserves him, someone who will love him properly.'

'Come on, you're not being fair on yourself. Who's to say I was right and you were wrong? Yeah, I met Chris, but not until I was nearly fifty, Kate. Too late for kids. I mean, it's worth it, don't get me wrong, it's worth it now, but it was a huge gamble and there was no guarantee it would pay off. I might still be on my own now, or still dating wanker after wanker off the internet, and you might still be with Dan, if you hadn't just had some weird romance thing going on with the hottest movie star on the planet that is, you might be looking forward to the boys going off to uni and more time together. Who knows? No one does, that's the point.'

There is nothing else to say or, at least, I have told her as much as I can. We finish the red and then the rose and half the white. Some time in the night she finds her way into the guest room, my room, and we are reversed. The room in the house that has been kept for my crazily recklessly perfectionist sister has somehow become mine. It might have taken the best part of half a century for our birth order to be realised but, for the first time in my life, I actually think of her as my 'big' sister – she is looking after me now. And I sleep at last. It is a wine induced, restless sleep, that will leave me in tatters tomorrow, but it is sleep.

FOURTEEN

I go to Paris. I do not plan to go to Paris, but I go to Paris anyway. Perhaps I always knew I would. I need to check my emails, get back to work, get my shit together and move out of my parents'. I need to find somewhere to live, somewhere for the boys to come and stay. I need to grow up. So I spend the best part of a day forcing myself to work through emails and admin. Sometime in the early evening I log out, and there it is – a headline on my newsfeed:

'James Talisker and Saskia Hamilton Engaged! Saskia recently joined James on the set of his new movie in Paris where, friends have disclosed, he surprised her with a shock proposal. The pair are said to be more in love than ever and plan to wed this summer in a small ceremony for select close friends and family.'

So, I go to Paris. I take the Eurostar. I have never felt sick on a train before, but I do on this one. It feels hot, claustrophobic, I can't wait to get off. The rising panic that became lodged in my chest when I read the article yesterday is still there. There is no way to release it.

I buy cigarettes from a kiosk outside the Gare du Nord. I haven't smoked in years. It seems I have forgotten. There's a paper on the stand with James's photo on the front so I buy that too. My schoolgirl French has all but deserted me but there is pull out inside with all the filming locations throughout the city. They are the ones you would expect really. I don't know what I'm doing here.

I make my way to the river, it is what I have done every time I have been to Paris. It is what I do everywhere, to make my way to water. I find somewhere to sit and light a cigarette. My hands are shaking. It takes three attempts with the matches I have bought. I take a tentative first drag, the second deeper one makes me cough. I start to feel lightheaded but carry on. Half-way through the cigarette I gag and, before I know it, I am retching and throwing up the remnants of lunch. Thank god it's winter.

I check into my hotel, business like. It is almost as if I am here working. Almost. I can't face a restaurant meal alone, so I go out for a walk instead. I grab some falafel from a street stall and walk, aimlessly. I don't know what I'm doing here. It's late, I'll start tomorrow.

I sleep with the curtains open. It is the first time I have stayed in a hotel room without him for months, and I wonder what he's doing, where he is, if one of the lights in the distance or nearby is his. A hotel room like mine, but not like mine. Or a party or reception somewhere. I feel calmer than I have in days, it is a relief just to be in the same city again. It will be ok. But then I remember that he is here with his girlfriend, his fiancée, and I do not know what I am doing here.

In the morning I feel nauseous again. I decide I must be hungry and take breakfast in the hotel, a proper breakfast. After that I walk up to Montmartre. It is the first of the locations in the paper. I move around to each one, never stopping to go in anywhere, just being where he has been.

Eventually I end up at Notre Dame, just as I knew I would. I know that this is where they are filming today. There is an area cordoned off right at the front of the cathedral and, this side of the barrier, a couple of hundred bystanders. But I would have known anyway. I hang back. I don't know why, it's not as if he's going to pick me out amongst all these people in any case. I don't know what I am doing here. A small group of actors emerge from the entrance, surrounded by what must be a larger group of crew. I can just about make him out. People around me are calling his name, trying to get his attention. Some are calling for the other actors, but mainly it's for him. Someone nudges me, gently, smiling. She says something in French I can't catch and gestures towards James, and then she puts her hands over her heart, in the same way that the waitress back in Holborn did, and sighs dramatically. 'He's not happy,' I find myself saying, out loud, and the woman looks at me quizzically. 'He's not happy,' I repeat.

I try to edge my way closer, slowly, I don't want to draw attention to myself. I don't want to draw attention to myself, and yet, I want him to see me, don't I? Isn't that why I'm here? I feel suddenly claustrophobic again, I have never liked crowds. People are pushing at me from all angles, I feel as if my feet might lift off the ground and I will just be carried along with them, like a leaf in the wind. I call out his name, and he seems to glance in my direction. For a moment I think he has heard me, but then I realise I have not spoken aloud at all. As the crowd surges again, I feel my phone vibrate inside my coat pocket. I pick up, allowing the crowd to move around and in front of me.

'Mum said you're in Paris.'

'Yes.'

'Christ, what's all that noise? Where are you?'

'Notre Dame.'

'This is a bad idea, Kate. You need to come home.'

I don't answer.

'Kate.'

I wait for her to hang up.

'It's not going to go well, Kate. There is only one way it can go. What are you even planning? Kate!'

I will get closer, I want to tell her, and then I will call his name and he will see me, and he will see I've followed him to Paris after all, just like he wanted me to. And it will be just as if the last few weeks have not happened at all. He'll come to my hotel room, and he'll put his arms around me and kiss me again, the way he used to, before I messed everything up. And I won't ask about her, I won't. He will tell me if he wants to, I'll let him, but I won't want him to, he'll know that. So what if he's getting married, nothing else has changed, has it? I will be a friend to him, just like he asked me to be in the beginning. And I can do that, can't I? I can be the friend he wanted me to be, a good friend, the best of friends. Anything, just so long as it's not nothing.

'Kate, what are you doing?'

'I don't know,' I tell her. 'I don't know what I'm doing here.'

And then I hang up, and I start to back away from the crowd, breaking free in seconds now that I am moving against the current.

So, I don't tell her how it will be, about how he will ask me to be brave one more time and that this time I won't hesitate. I don't tell her that this is the bit I have been running in my head, just below the level of conscious thought, ever since I saw his name in the news the day before yesterday. I don't tell her that he's been just as miserable without me as I have been without him, that anyone could see that just by looking at him. Anyone who knows him, that is. I don't tell her that it will all be ok now, that we'll fix it, it was just a misunderstanding that we'll fix now.

And what would she have said if I had told her? That I was delusional, that whatever there had been between me and James, if there ever was anything in the first place, was over now, and who would know anyway if he was acting then or acting now, it's his job after all. No, she wouldn't say all that. She would think it, all of it, but she wouldn't say it. She would be worried about me, she is worried about me. 'Just come home,' she would say. 'Just come home before you get hurt.'

Isn't that what she's already said anyway?

I find a pharmacy that will give me something to help me sleep, something that will be taken alongside half a bottle of wine, later. There are some bottles of the aftershave James advertises scattered across the counter display and, on a whim, I pick one up. But, when I break it open that evening, cloaking myself and the hotel room in unfamiliar notes, I realise it is not the scent he wears in real life at all. It is as if I have opened the door to a stranger. In the morning, my cheeks are blotchy, and my eyes are swollen and stiff with the mascara I did not remove last night. I have a feeling that, if I have not implemented a strict cleanse, tone, moisturise regime by now, I probably never will. It is the first time I have ever admitted this to myself, I realise. I try not to think about how many other things there are that are too late to change now. There is a feeling in my throat as if I have been crying, though I do not remember it. I will go home today but I will go to the Louvre first. It was not on the list of filming locations outlined in the paper.

I do not gravitate to the Mona Lisa, but to the depths below – to the part of the Louvre I fell in love with first as a teenager, the sculpture rooms. There is a part of me that is fantasising still that he will somehow materialise in here, as if in a film. That we will have been inexplicably drawn to the exact same spot at the exact same time, to the one location that ought to have been used in his film but has not been. I have followed him all the way to Paris and yet I am still waiting for him to come to me, to find me. But, if this was a film, I would be an extra, a faceless blur in a crowd, devoid of backstory, a transparency without a negative. It's not what Zoe would have done, even if she had told me to come home. Zoe would have pushed to the front of that crowd, made him hear her, made him see her. Zoe would have made something happen, kicking and screaming, she would have made something happen. But I am not my sister. We see you, the sculptures seem to whisper, you are still enough for us, and they envelop me in their cooling embrace.

On the Eurostar, I write him a letter, a proper handwritten letter on paper. When I get home, I will take an envelope and a stamp from Mum's bureau in the dining room and I will put it in a post box and send it to him care of his agent's office, and then I will draw a line under it, and I will try and forget about it for a while. Perhaps, one day, I will be able to look back on those few months with fondness, like when someone you love has died and eventually you learn to smile at all the unexpectedly little memories of them doing banal things – like poaching an egg, or shaving at the kitchen sink, rinsing out a worn razor in the washing up bowl. You hope that the memories will last longer than the pain, it is the most you might expect. You do not expect it even, but it is possible it will happen, and that has to be enough for now.

I write that I am sorry, and that I know now he was better than me in all the ways I could not see as well as in all the ways that I could. I tell him that I hope he will forgive me one day, and that my heart will be a little bit less broken if he can and, though I don't deserve him to care, I know that he will anyway. I tell him that, even though I always expected it to end, I never expected to stop loving him. I will always be his friend if he wants me, I am not going anywhere. And then, because I know that I should, I wish him all the best for his marriage, and I hope he'll be happy, in that and in everything else. I do not tell him that I came to Paris.

FIFTEEN

Karl asks if we can meet. He says he will come to me, and I arrange to pick him up from the station. It might have seemed strange before, meeting up with him outside of college, but nothing does anymore, so I barely even register it as anything out of the ordinary until I'm actually standing at the entrance waiting for him.

'Kate! God, I've missed you,' is the first thing he says, pulling me into a bear hug and kissing me on both cheeks.

'I've missed you too,' and, as I say it, I suddenly realise it's true and my voice catches slightly on the words.

I drive us to the seafront, and we find a tea room with huge steamed up windows to huddle away from the wind in. He asks me about work first, and I try and answer enthusiastically, like I would have done before. He makes all the right noises back, but I can tell there's something more coming, I can feel the wait.

'So, I'm not going to be your teacher anymore.'

'I know.'

'But I hope that this will be the start of a new relationship for us, a more equal one. I'd like us to be friends, Kate.'

'I'd like that too.'

Again, it's true. I'm not sure it would have seemed possible to me before, I think I would have always looked up to him somehow, and it would have got in the way. I will still look up to him, of course, but the gap between us doesn't seem as huge as it once did. It's close enough for us to be friends now. I don't know if it's because of James, or the installations, or maybe it's something of both.

'But, if we're going to be friends, we have to be honest with one another, don't we? Say the things that it might not be comfortable to hear sometimes.'

I nod. I'm not sure where this is going.

'The thing is, Kate, well, there's been some rumours – I'm sure you know. Anyway, I don't care about any of that – well, unless you want to talk about it, that is. But Jessica asked me if you were ok…'

'She shouldn't have done that.'

'She didn't say anything other than that. Obviously, she's your agent now, and no one will have your back like she will, I promise. But we're friends, and she knows that we're still in touch. I just got the impression she was a bit worried about you, that's all.'

'I'm fine.'

'Do you want to talk about it?'

'I don't think I would really know where to start... I don't know – look, the main thing is I'm getting divorced, and I'm back living with my parents again. I'm not sure I want to talk about the other stuff.'

'About James Talisker, you mean?'

'Whatever it was, it's over.'

'Well, that's your business anyway – it's your work I'm concerned about.'

It's like the conversation I had with Dan all over again – except what Karl means by work and what Dan meant by work are completely different. At first, I feel myself bristle at the intrusion, but this is tempered by the awareness that, next to myself, Karl probably cares more about my work than anyone.

'You don't need to worry.'

'I hope not. It's just I know how hard you've worked to get to this point, how much you've sacrificed even. I mean, whatever has happened with James Talisker... Well, I suspect your marriage being over is more a consequence of your work than that.'

I nod. It's true.

'The installations you've had, and the new exhibition you've got coming up, I'm not going to say it's luck – god knows, you've earned it. But these are once in a lifetime opportunities, Kate – you might not get them again if you don't make the most of them now.'

I don't know what to tell him – that for a moment there I didn't care? That I was hardly even thinking of my own kids, let alone my career. That Dan was right, I am pathetic. That everything I am feeling is worse because I only have myself to blame. That I hate myself even for the things I have no control over. That I still lie under the covers in my sister's bed, curled up in a ball, sobbing, day after day, night after night, sobbing but all the time repressing the scream that it isn't fair. It isn't fair, like a child. It isn't fair that I have fallen in love with someone I can't have. It isn't fair that he doesn't love me back. It isn't fair that I am too old, and he is too young. It isn't fair that I am not the sort of woman a famous actor could be with, would be with, should be with. It isn't fair that I am so ordinary, so normal, and that other people exist in this world who are so extraordinary, so exceptional. It isn't fair that, if I were a man, none of this would matter. It isn't fair that it matters to me even though it shouldn't.

'I know,' is all I say. 'I'm trying.'

If it wasn't true before, it has to be now.

Back at the station, Karl smiles shyly, and hesitates slightly as he says goodbye. There is something else he wants to tell me, I'm sure.

'So, I guess, since you haven't said anything, you haven't heard my news?'

I shake my head.

'I thought everyone had heard by now but, well, I suppose you've been busy, you're not as up on all the gossip as you would usually be.'

I feel a stab of guilt at this. I've not been in touch with anyone from college almost since the opening night of the installation. It feels like a lifetime ago now.

'What is it?'

'Finn's moving in. This weekend actually. I hope – we hope – you'll visit soon, come and stay? We'll go out, try and cheer you up a bit.'

'Crikey, I had no idea you two were even a couple. How the hell did I miss that one?'

'We weren't. It wouldn't have been right – while he was still a student, and while I was still his teacher, you know? But, anyway, he's not now and I'm not and – well, what can I say, we're in love I guess. There didn't seem much point in trying to hide it anymore.'

His happiness is infectious, almost bursting out of

him now that I finally see it, and I am so relieved that I can still feel it. That, in spite of everything that has happened, I can still be happy for someone else, for two wonderful friends that have found one another. That this bitterness I feel has not yet poisoned every last part of me.

'Life's short, Kate. Don't stop making things happen for yourself, now that you've started.'

'I won't,' I say. 'I promise.'

But it's a hollow promise because it was broken before I even made it.

Mum is in the kitchen when I get back, waiting – though she does not say it. She looks older this last week or so, but perhaps that is my doing.

I give her a kiss on the cheek and say thank you.

'For what?'

'Oh, you know, for letting me stay, for not asking too many questions…'

'I've been worried.'

'I know.'

I wonder how much Zoe has told her.

'Try not to though. I will be ok. And the boys are fine too, with Dan.'

She nods, unconvinced.

'Actually, I'm taking them to look at flats tomorrow, after school. Can't stay here forever, can I?'

I regret it almost as soon as I have said it – I will have no choice but to book viewings now. But perhaps it's a good thing after all, it's a start at least.

We look at three flats, but the boys have decided on the one they want before we have even seen any of them. It is the one I like least, but it is close to town, and that seems to be the deciding factor for them.

'It won't be forever,' I warn them. 'I'm probably going to buy something at some stage, and I don't really want to buy round here.'

'But you're getting us keys cut though?' Max asks.

'Yes, of course, and you'll have your own room each to do what you want with. It's up to you how often you stay here, or if you want to move in, or stay with Dad, or whatever. You're old enough to make your own minds up now.'

'I'm not sure yet,' Josh is characteristically hesitant. 'I might stay at Dad's, for now. It's ok though, the flat – I like it more than I thought I would.'

I take a step towards him. I want to take him in my arms and hold him there for too long, until he breaks free. But I don't. It will make him uncomfortable. I cannot even remember the last time one of them came to me for a hug, for comfort. Those times have been and gone almost as quickly as the family home has become 'Dad's'.

'I'm sorry it's turned out this way,' I say. 'Things will be better now though, from now on.'

I take them for burgers after, and then drop them back at the house. It feels strange, going back, from the outside looking in. I should have been back already, to pick up the rest of my stuff, but I couldn't face it.

'Dad said to ask when you're coming back for your stuff?' Max asks, as if reading my mind.

'You can tell him I've got the flat now,' I say. 'I'll pick up the rest of my things as soon as I get the keys.'

I wait for them to go in before reversing off the drive and out onto the road again. The light is on in the lounge and I can see Dan watching me from the window as I switch into first. I lift my hand to him, in a kind of salute, but he lets the curtain drop back down again without acknowledging me. It seems to me then almost as if I don't know him at all, and I don't know if this is the illusion or the fact that, just a few short weeks ago, he was still my husband.

SIXTEEN

The phone vibrating on the bedside cabinet next to me cuts into my sleep. I miss the call but see that Zoe has rung three times already. Just as I'm thinking about ringing her back, the phone vibrates again in my hand. As soon as I pick up she's talking.

'Kate, it's James Talisker.'

'Yeah, I know, he's getting married.'

Even as I say it, I know it's not that – Zoe would not ring me at this time in the morning just to tell me that.

'No, it's not that. He's in hospital, back in London. I didn't know whether to tell you, but you would've seen it sooner or later anyway, and I thought it would be better if you heard it from me first. They're saying he tried to take his own life, Kate. He might not make it…'

I don't look up what hospital he's in until I'm already on the train. I'll work out what tube to get on the way. I resist looking for as long as I can. I know the internet will be full of it, and I'm not sure yet how much of it I'm prepared to see. I don't know how much of it I can cope with and still function. I haven't even thought about what I'm going to do when I get there. I can't think about it. Somehow, I know he will want me there. I don't know how I know it, I can't explain it. It is just something I feel somewhere below conscious thought.

I look on BBC News first. It doesn't go into too much detail, thankfully, only that he was found by neighbours in the early hours of this morning and admitted to an undisclosed London hospital. His family have asked for privacy at this time. I will have to look on the gossip pages if I want to find out where he is.

'Actor James Talisker was found unconscious out-side his London flat in the early hours of Thurs-day morning. An unnamed source confirmed that his long-term girlfriend, Saskia Hamilton, left the flat for good earlier this week and friends of the couple now fear the worst. A spokesperson con-firmed that James is currently receiving treatment at St Cedd's Hospital, London, and close family are thought to be in attendance.'

There is more, but I close it down. It makes me feel sick reading it. It makes me feel sick at myself to think that, just a few months ago, I would have read all of it, consumed all of it, a life reduced to 'content'. I think about Dan looking out at me from the window, about how he seemed like a stranger to me then, and it is the complete opposite of how I feel thinking about James now. It is as if all the content of my own life has become displaced and uncatalogued somehow, and it has been beyond my capabilities to reorder, or even to make sense, of it. Everything has been pulled out to the middle, and all I can do is step around it.

Press are blocking the main entrance to the hospital – mostly photographers, but also a couple of what look like film crews. There are other groups hanging around too, fans I suppose. It makes me angry, but then I remember I'm no better than any of them, that I have no right to be here either. I think about trying to pick my way through, but then I see they have security guards on the door – checking appointment details and letters. The thought that I might not even be able to get through the entrance had not even occurred to me. If I had been thinking about anything on the way, it was about how I was going to get past the front desk.

I do a circuit of the main hospital building and find a smaller side entrance. There is a security guard there too, just one, but it's much quieter here and hopefully he'll let me by. He asks me if I have an appointment letter, and I tell him I've forgotten it, left it at home, but I'm just here for a scan – I know where I'm going. He tells me he's not supposed to let anyone in without a letter.

'It's usually fine,' I say. 'What's going on today anyway?'

This must seem convincing enough, and he waves me in.

'Some actor,' he calls after me, as I try to look as if I do know where I'm going. 'Overdose, or something.'

Once I get further into the hospital, I know there will be signs directing me back to the main entrance. I follow them round until I reach the reception area, and can see the buzz of people outside. Then there's that panicky feeling rising in my chest again, and I start to feel faint. I wonder if this is what the start of a heart attack feels like. I try to approach the front desk as if I have every legitimate reason to be here, and tell the woman quietly that I'm here to see James Talisker.

'Sorry, who?' she asks. 'I didn't catch that. Do you have your hospital number handy?'

'I'm not here for an appointment,' I say. 'I'm here to see a friend – James Talisker. I'm not sure what ward he's been admitted to.'

She frowns. 'I can only give that sort of information out to immediate family. You'll have to make contact via them, I'm afraid.'

She's trying to be polite, but I can sense her impatience. Perhaps she thinks I'm a reporter.

'I am a friend – a real friend, I mean. I'm not a journalist.'

'Oh, I know,' she says. 'It's just the rules though – sorry.'

'Well, can you get a message to him then? If you tell him who it is, he'll tell you it's fine, I promise.'

'You'd really have to go through the family for that – sorry.'

'I can't – I don't know them. Look, I know him, but I don't know his family. They don't know me, they won't have heard of me.'

'Well, if you are friends, I'm sure you'll be able to get a message to him somehow...'

She glances to her left slightly, and then to the front entrance. She must be trying to get the attention of the security guards.

'Please,' I say, knowing how desperate I must sound. 'I know what it looks like. Can you just find out if he's ok for me? As soon as I know he's ok, I'll go, I promise. But I can't go until I know he's ok – I just have to know he's ok is all.'

There's a queue forming behind me now, and I hear someone a couple of spaces back tut and sigh. My cheeks are burning and the tears I have held back all morning are pricking my eyes and making my head thud. There are people looking on from both sides now. An older couple and their daughter, nervously glancing back and forth between the front entrance and the reception desk, as if they are waiting for something to happen, to my right. A woman with a buggy, and a man in a wheelchair, to my left.

'I'm sorry,' the woman repeats. 'We can only give that kind of information out to immediate family members.'

There is more of an edge of finality to her voice this time, and she must have made some kind of signal to the security guards, as one of them is approaching now. I turn to face him and, as I do, the woman glances again to her left, to where the older couple and their daughter are standing. She seems to smile slightly, apologetically, in their direction.

'It's ok,' I say. 'I'm going.'

I say it a little too loudly and I can just about make out a stifled giggle from somewhere in the room. The security guard moves slowly, as if to take my arm.

'Let me show you out,' he says, gently.

'It's fine, you don't need to. I'm going.'

I push past the queue, past the other security guards on the door, and the crowd outside, and then I run – out from the hospital grounds, and onto the street. I need to find somewhere to sit down. I'm feeling really faint now. The beads of sweat that have collected on my upper lip seem to cool and freeze as they meet the outside air, so that I feel strangely hot and cold at the same time. I feel a wave of pain at my core. It is worse than how I felt the morning he left me, worse than in Paris, it is a physical pain ripping through my body like a pulse. I reach out my hand to try and find something, anything, to grip onto. There is a walled flower bed a metre or so away. I sink down, thinking I will be able to rest my back against it and get my breath. But I have sat too far away, and only my upper back makes contact. My fingers are tingling. I tell myself I'm hyperventilating, to breathe, you're having a panic attack is all. I hear someone calling my name through the mist of nausea, but there is no one there, there can't be. I don't want to open my eyes. If I open my eyes, everything will spin out of control. Everything is already spinning out of control.

'Kate? It is Kate, isn't it?'

She sounds like she's been running. I force myself to open my eyes and look up. It is the woman from the hospital, the one who was with the older couple. I try to nod. She looks vaguely familiar to me, but I can't quite place her. I think that she must be someone I know from somewhere out of context, but then what would the context be for this?

'I thought it was you. It's ok, you don't know me.'

She must have sensed my disconnect.

'I'm Lily – James's sister.'

'Oh God,' I'm trying to speak. 'Oh God,' I want to say. 'Is he ok?' but my words are slurring, and I can't seem to get my mouth to form around them in the way that it should.

'I recognised you – you probably don't remember – I dropped him off once to meet you. At your hotel? He has a photo of you still on his phone... Are you, are you ok?'

I try to nod again. My legs feel strangely warm, damp. I look down at them, my knees pulled up to my chest, just like in Pembrokeshire. And then my mouth works, and I say the words as soon as I think them, there is no filter.

'I think I'm having a miscarriage.'

'Christ, ok. Right, we need to get you back inside then – now.'

All hesitancy is gone from her voice now, and I am grateful for it. I feel like I cannot even function through the pain at the moment, and that is only the physical pain.

Somehow we make it back to the entrance, I am leaning against her and she is half dragging me to the doorway. They start to ask for an appointment letter as we approach, but she hisses at them under her breath.

'She's having a fucking miscarriage.'

And then I'm being lowered into a wheelchair and pushed somewhere, A&E maybe, I don't know. I feel like I'm conscious but there are pieces missing, portholes of nothingness amongst all the chaos. Do we see the older couple again as we go in? They must be James's parents, I realise.

I'm made to lie on a bed, or a trolley. It must be a trolley because I'm being wheeled into different places. There are examinations, scans. There is a lot of blood, red against white. I retreat to a place inside of myself, to where there was a baby, maybe still is a baby. I want to find her in there, to connect with her before she goes. My baby, his baby, not a miscarriage, not a foetus, a baby. People are saying my name, telling me to wake up. They are looking through my bag, though my purse.

'Zoe,' I try to say. 'Don't call Dan – call Zoe.'

But the words aren't working again. I don't want to wake up. I won't find her in consciousness, my baby, she will be down there somewhere underneath.

'I'm here,' I want to tell her. 'I've come for you.'

Someone is shaking me – a doctor?

'We need to take you down to theatre now,' he is

telling me.

'We need to take her now,' he repeats, turning to someone standing in the doorway. 'It's really important we don't waste any more time.'

She nods, pale faced, and, as they wheel me past her, she takes my hand, briefly, lifts it to her lips, kisses it. Who is that?

'Take care, Kate,' she says.

And then I remember – James's sister Lily, she is still here.

She is the first person I see when I wake up, still standing there in the doorway. It can't be the same room, can it?

'Hey, Kate,' she says, gently. 'How are you feeling now?'

'Better,' I say. 'Not quite so shaky. Still not quite with it though. I'm sorry I put you through that.'

'It's fine. I'm just glad you're ok.'

'Please tell me how James is?'

'He's doing ok too. We were worried, at first, but he'll be fine, I promise. Mum and Dad are with him. I need to get back there, I just wanted to make sure you were ok.'

'And the baby?'

I already know the answer, don't I? It's why I didn't

ask about her first. She shakes her head.

'I'm so sorry, Kate. The doctors will explain it all properly. Do you want me to call anyone for you?'

I shake my head.

'I'll call my sister,' I say. 'She'll come straight away. I'll be fine.'

'Kate, I have to ask you, was James… was James the father? Was it my brother's?'

I can't answer her, the words will choke me.

'Please don't tell him.'

She doesn't answer me at first and, when she does, it is measured, considered.

'I can't promise you that. I'm sorry. I don't know what the best thing to do is yet. I need to wait and see how he is first. I won't be telling him today though.'

'It's ok, I know how you must be feeling. You don't need to stay with me.'

'Look, Kate, I don't know what went on between you and my brother, but I know you meant something to him. Might still mean something to him even. I do know that. But you obviously came here today for a reason, and I'm just not sure it's the right time. Just let him get better first, yeah? And maybe wait 'til you're better too?'

I suddenly feel really tired. She's been kind but I don't want her here anymore. She isn't here for me, she's here for James. I want Zoe.

'You don't need to worry,' I say. 'I'm not going to try and get in and see him again.'

My voice is cracking now, I can't help it.

'I just needed to know that he was ok, is all. There was all this stuff on the internet saying he'd tried to kill himself, that he might not make it… I couldn't find anything out, they wouldn't tell me anything. But if you're telling me he's ok now, I'll leave it. You wouldn't be in here, would you, with me, if he wasn't? I'm not, I'm not…'

I'm not, what? Not some kind of weird stalker, when all the evidence points to the contrary. I wonder how many mad fans she's had try to door-step her in the past. She crosses to the bed, takes my hand again.

'Hey, please don't be upset, I really didn't mean to upset you. I'm sorry, I know you must care about him too, of course you do. Look, just concentrate on getting yourself better for now, that's all I'm saying. And then maybe, when you're both all fixed up again… well, who knows?'

She turns back to face me from the doorway, and I force my face to crease into a smile. She looks as if there's something else she wants to say, changes her mind, and then changes it back again.

'And Kate, do yourself a favour, yeah? And him. Just try not to believe everything you read about my brother in the papers?'

SEVENTEEN

I lie on the bed waiting for Zoe to come. The stitches are painful, and I'm wary of turning onto my side, or of doing anything that will put too much pressure on them. I am focusing on the physical pain for now, nurturing it almost, because it is the only thing keeping me from what is beyond it. When Zoe gets here, you can allow yourself to feel, I think, just wait for Zoe.

When she does come, she doesn't say anything at first, and I am grateful for it. She lies down on the tiny hospital bed beside me, and I nestle my head against her shoulder. She takes my hand and I begin to cry, and then we are both crying together. We are crying for this baby, for my baby, for the loss of the life she would have lived, and for what she would have been to both of us, but we are crying for Zoe too, for all the children she will never have, might have had once, but now never will.

After a while, she says she will book into a nearby hotel for the night, if I'm going to be ok, that is. I am going to be ok, I tell her. I tell her what the doctor told me, after Lily left – that I'd had an ectopic pregnancy, that there was nothing they could do to save the baby, nothing that anyone could have done, that they'd had to operate, I'd lost a lot of blood, there'd been a transfusion, but I was fine now, I would be fine now.

'Well, if you're sure.'

She doesn't sound convinced.

That night I dream I am trailing a hedgerow along the side of a field, and a child skips just ahead of me, to my right. She turns to me and smiles, and the sun picks out the auburn highlights in her hair as she does so. But she is always just ahead of me, no matter how fast I go, and I find I cannot reach her, no matter how hard I try. I begin to tire, and the gap between us widens. I am worried that something will happen to her, something outside of my control, that she will become lost, or that someone might take her perhaps. And then she is no longer there, and I become disorientated. At first, I search frantically, in a ditch at the boundary between this field and the next, and then behind a cattle trough over on the far side but, after a time, I begin to wonder if she was ever here at all, if she wasn't just something my mind had invented. The memory of her is hazed, and tinged with the knowledge that she may not have existed at all or, worse still, that she did, and I am forgetting her already.

Another memory is returning. I am back on the trolley. The scan is showing a pregnancy, they say – not a baby, a pregnancy. But I can see her on the screen, my baby, and I know she is a girl, just as surely as I knew Max and Josh were boys when I first saw them on hospital scans too. She has her father's jawline, I think, but it will look different on a girl. I think I may say it aloud, but my words do not seem to carry any currency in this room – perhaps I am already sedated.

The two images shift in my mind – the girl in the field and the baby on the scan. I no longer know which is real, and which a dream, but she evaporates before me anyway. The harder I search for her, the more she eludes me. It is like trying to catch mist in your hand – as soon as you feel it, it's gone.

The hospital chaplain comes to see me to explain how the cremations work. We will attend a service alongside other families, she says, for all the babies. Each baby will have its own casket, but they will all go in together.

'And afterwards?' I ask.

'For afterwards, we have a garden of remembrance

– the ashes are scattered there. It's usually about a month or so after the service. It's beautiful, a really peaceful place to be. You wouldn't even know you're in a hospital. And you're welcome to come and sit there any time, for however long you want to. But it's completely up to you, of course, all families grieve differently.'

'But how... how will you know whose is whose?'

'I'm sorry?'

'The babies – how will you know which one was mine? Which one is her? My baby.'

'We don't... we can't separate them out, I'm afraid. It's not possible.'

She looks across to Zoe for help, and I await my sister's intervention. She makes her choice in an instant.

'I'm not sure that's going to be the best thing here,' she says, somewhat hesitantly.

I know her better than anyone though – this hesitancy is all politeness, there is a steeliness underneath that only I can determine. I breathe a sigh of relief inwards. Zoe understands, Zoe will make it right, Zoe will know what to do.

'It's all done very nicely,' the chaplain is explaining, reassuring. 'Most families do find it brings some comfort. You might not feel like it now but, if you don't attend the service, at least, you may wish you had done so later.'

'No, I'm so sorry, I've not been very clear, have I? We would like our own service for my sister's baby. We prefer to keep it separate. My sister would like to take her baby's ashes away with her afterwards, and she's not comfortable with the way you usually do it. That's all.'

'We do sometimes make separate arrangements for special circumstances,' the chaplain is wavering slightly. 'But only very occasionally...'

'We understand. If there is an additional charge, we'll be more than happy to pay it – whatever it is.'

'Thank you,' I say to her, after the woman has left.

'Honestly, Kate, just don't worry about it – it's the least I can do.'

'I don't know how I'm supposed to feel,' I say.

Everything inside is so loud at the moment, condensed, and it's making it hard to separate any of it out, just like all those babies' ashes, to make sense of it.

'Do you want me to tell Dan?' Zoe is asking.

'She wasn't his.'

'No, I realise. You don't want me to tell...'

'No.'

'Ok, it's your choice. Maybe it's for the best anyway.'

'Maybe.'

The service is short. I have not asked for readings or music, beyond what they would usually offer. The chaplain seems almost disappointed, almost as if we should be getting our money's worth, now that we have put them to all this extra trouble.

I do not cry. Zoe does, but I do not. I do hold her hand though, I grip her fingers as if she is tethering me to the earth itself, and I don't think I have ever loved her as much as I do in this moment. It is a cliché, a verse you might find printed inside a card, but she is the best friend I have ever had and the only one I have ever needed. I push the thought away again as soon as it comes – I can't allow myself to think about it now. If I think too much about her being here, I might have to consider the possibility that one day she may not be. It's not a possibility I can bear to visit today, when having her here beside me is the only thing keeping me upright.

For a moment it is as if James is here beside me too, almost as if the cracks between different outcomes are opening up, splitting apart and reforming again, exposing something that might once have existed in the future. I do not know if he ever did really love me, it is possible he did for a moment in time, but he would have loved her – I do know that. I see us together in the field and, this time when she runs, he calls after her to wait. Where I struggled to keep pace with her before, he reaches her easily, swinging her up, squealing, into his arms. They turn back to face me, smiling, laughing, splintered sunlight on auburn. And then they are gone.

EIGHTEEN

I book to go to Antarctica. I always thought that, when I eventually went, I would go at the very beginning of the season, when everything was intact, pristine. I have never liked dirty snow. But, now that it comes to it, I find I do not care at all that it's the wrong time – it somehow feels like the right thing to do anyway. I do not feel guilty about leaving the boys behind – Antarctica has always been my dream, and they have never understood my yearning to go, much less feel it also.

So, I pack up my daughter's ashes, still in the little container the hospital gave them to me in, and I set sail. I do not take a camera with me, or even a phone, but I do take the sun compass James gave me and the ring. I have not worn the ring since the night he gave it to me – it has been stowed behind the sun compass, in the battered wooden box, ever since. Sometimes I take it out, twisting it in the sunlight, and wonder what it would be like to wear it every day – an engagement ring, but not an engagement ring. It is a scab that I cannot help but pick. His face is blurring now, but the pain is not. I could look at pictures of him online, I could watch him on screen, even develop the photo I took of him in Pembrokeshire, but I won't – it would feel like cheating somehow. Instead, I allow his features to lose a little shape in my mind, because that feels real, makes what I felt feel real. But my fingertips will never forget the line of his jaw, replicated in hers.

I have not spoken about her with anyone, not even Zoe, since the hospital. I have never been the sort of person to go to others for help, never understood how their sympathy could make me feel anything other than worse, how the awkwardness of a comforting arm could ever bring solace. But that is not why I do not speak to anyone about her. I do not speak to anyone about her because I have an unshakeable belief that, if I do, she will become diluted in some way, as if she will evaporate along with my words in the air, just as she does in my dreams, and I am not yet ready to surrender her. I am not sure I will ever be. I am not yet ready to release the pain either. I do not want to tell myself that I need to stay positive, and all of those other banal platitudes we tell one another, and I want to hear them from others still less – I want to feel it, all of it, for as long as possible.

So, I cannot let go of him either – I can allow his

features to soften in my mind, but not the pain of losing him in my gut. I want to. I hate myself for it – that I still feel that first loss almost as keenly as this new one. It disgusts me. The shame of it churns in my stomach alongside the sickness that the Drake Crossing brings. But there is no edge to either pain, no boundary to either, so that the two have become intertwined within me. If I let go of one, I must let go of the other, if I let go of him I must let go of her. And, perhaps unthinkably, that I might eventually have to let go of her in order to let go of him. It is not a deal I feel I will ever be able to broker.

And yet, it is what I have come here to do, or what I have come here to start to do anyway, and it is also the reason why it has to be here. Even as I tell myself I can't do it, that I will never be able to do it, I somehow know that I will, that I will have to, that I will let them go together, that I will find a way to begin to, at least. I just don't yet know how.

After the sickness, there is an emptiness that is experienced as relief. It might only last for a moment, but it nevertheless comes whether you expect it to or not. You begin to hope that the emptiness might last a little longer each time, so that eventually there will be more emptiness than sickness. But that is rarely how it works, and that is the risk and the danger of hope, I suppose. And then, one day, the waters calm and the relief does not come from emptiness, but from that – only from that. The emptiness is on the outside now. This is the emptiness I have travelled to the bottom of the world to find.

I am the only single person in our party. The rest are couples or families. None of the kids are small – I think the youngest must be about thirteen. I don't mind. I am relieved not to have any pressure to 'pair up' with anyone. I enjoy the trips on the sea kayaks the most, and the feeling of insignificance that comes from the brush of my smallness against the vastness of it all. That the closer you get, the smaller you seem. It's a reassurance to me – this idea that everything I am and do is so ultimately inconsequential. I wonder what it would feel like to be the sort of person who felt the opposite, to be the sort of person who found the thought of that more terrifying than a comfort. At first, I can't understand why James wanted someone else to share it with, all those years ago, and I wonder briefly if he was the second type of person after all – the sort who would be terrified by it – but I know he is not. He seeks to lose himself in bigger things the same way that I do. He was lucky to have come here so young, I think, to be given that freedom from self in time to make the most of it. And then I realise that it wasn't that he had wanted to find someone else to share it with back then, in the sense that he would seek them out, it was more that he had realised or hoped that one day he would somehow come to know the someone he would want to share it with anyway, the some-one that he could disappear alongside, readily – the someone he would cling to, and who would cling to him, until the moment the ship crashed, and beyond.

One day we visit a post office in a souvenir shop, or a souvenir shop in a post office – I'm not entirely sure which. I find a postcard and write it out to the boys:

'You were right – it's freezing! The penguins are worth it though. Will take you somewhere warm in the Summer, I promise. Love you, Mum x'

I will see them before the postcard, but it doesn't matter – that's not the reason I'm sending it. I send it to stay connected, to stay tethered. It's a self-indulgence to be here, I know that. I've always put them first before – tried to at least – but, in the end, it wasn't enough, I haven't quite turned out to be enough of the parent I thought I'd be. I will have to be a better one after this. James must have stood in this same shop when he was about Max's age, and I wonder now if Max thinks about future loves in the same way that James did back then. I hope me and Dan haven't lowered his expectations too much. It would be unforgiveable if he settled for something like we had, just because he thought that was all there was, unforgiveable if his life were to follow the same pattern. But then, surely that is the one thing even the worst of us gift to our children? Such proximity to our failings that, whatever mistakes they do make, they are determined not to repeat ours.

I wait until the last night to go up on deck alone. The light is not exactly as James described it, but he must have come earlier in the season. It is still not completely dark though, more blue than black. I sit there for a while, holding the tiny container carefully in both hands. I want to be still when I do this, I don't want to rush it. I want to breathe, and take my time, and get it right. I want to process the life she would have had. I see her as a toddler, as she was in the field, and then I allow my thoughts to run on to her first day at school, reports and awards to be proud of, friends, playdates, sleepovers, A-Levels, the uni years. I see her at work, on her wedding day, as a parent herself, beautiful, playful, confident, determined, resilient – a sister, an aunt. All the things she might have been and all the things she might never have been. The images blur and overlap, some stronger than others, approaching and receding in waves. Her hair sometimes long, sometimes pixie short, sparking in the light. Always that same jawline but, I only just see it now, my eyes – not grey, not his, but mine.

Eventually it is time, and I move slowly and cautiously to the side of the boat. I would have had to let her go if she had lived. There would have come a time when she would no longer have needed me, when I would have needed her more, when I would have had to accept that she was an adult and knew best how to live her own life. Not a goodbye – a good luck. I will have to do it for Max and Josh one day soon too, I realise. So, I let the wind carry her out and over the sea and, in the end, I do it willingly. I close my eyes, and I see her one last time – smiling back at me over her shoulder, glinting extraordinary as she goes, flying towards whale song and freedom.

NINETEEN

When I get back to the flat, there is a franked envelope waiting for me. It is a note from James's agent, with my letter from the train enclosed, unopened:

Thank you for writing to James Talisker, care of this agency. I regret to inform you, however, that Mr Talisker has requested we no longer forward any correspondence on from you. We are therefore returning your letter, as per his instructions, and must advise you that any future correspondence will also be returned.

I read it through twice, cheeks burning – this time in anger though, not in shame. Fuck him, I think, and then I say it again, aloud this time, and chuck the whole lot in the recycling bin. 'Fuck him.'

Dan asks if we can go for a walk. We take the path up through the woods to the ruins of the old manor house. The track is sodden and boggy with blackened wood mud, and we have to tread cautiously so that it seems to take forever. My feet, in thick socks and wellies, are heavy and trudging. It is much quieter than it would be on a weekend and, when we reach the top, we take a seat on a fallen tree trunk beside what is left of the original garden wall. He has brought tea. He silently pours some into the plastic cup from the top of the flask, and passes it to me. I can taste the Tupperware of childhood as I sip it.

'There's something I need to tell you,' he says.

'Ok.'

'I'm getting married again, once the divorce comes though. I've met someone.'

'Ok,' I say again. 'That's sudden.'

'Yeah. I haven't told the boys yet – I'm not sure how they'll take it. Anyway, I wanted to tell you first – in case they want to come and stay with you for a bit.'

'That's fine.'

'We need to sort the money out too. I know you said you didn't want anything, but I want it to be fair.'

I am surprised at this. He has always been rather mean where money is concerned but, then again, perhaps I'm not being as fair to him as he is to me – he has never been one to shirk responsibility.

'Unless...'

'Unless what?'

'Well, unless you wanted to give it another go, I suppose.'

He rushes this, so I realise then it is what he has asked me here to say.

'Do you want to?'

'I thought maybe we should.'

'I don't think that's the right reason to, do you?'

'I don't know. We've been married a long time.'

'What about this new person? Are you in love with her?'

'Yes, I think so – yes.'

'Well, that's your answer then.'

I can feel the irritation starting to swell in me. What does he want? My permission. It's not that even – he just wants it to be my fault, so he can say he was prepared to make it work even when I wasn't. But then, just as soon as the anger rises, it dissipates. I don't have to be pissed off with him anymore. We are free of one another now. And isn't it a good thing if he's happy? It's one less thing on my conscience – that I haven't ruined his life too. That, even after all those wasted years with me, he has found someone to love after all. So, I turn to him and smile.

'Dan, it's fine,' I can hear myself saying. 'Honestly, I don't want to get back together – not in the slight-

est. And I'm pleased you've found someone – genuinely.'

The relief is palpable.

'Really?'

'Yes, really – be happy. But you don't need my permission. Just be happy anyway.'

'Ok then.'

'Ok.'

We do not need to tread so carefully on the way
back down to the car, and I think perhaps we talk
more now, properly talk, than we have done in
years. He asks me about Antarctica, and seems
genuinely interested in the little snippets I tell
him. It's nice to have him listen, it feels like a reso-
lution of sorts.

'You went on your own then?'

'Yes, you know I went on my own.'

He nods. 'I'm glad you got to go finally – I mean,
I know you've always wanted to. Maybe we'll both
be happier now?'

'Maybe.'

'So, it didn't work out then? With the actor?'

'No, it didn't work out.'

'Well, probably for the best anyway.'

'Yes, probably.'

The gate to the car park is swinging open when we get back, and Dan closes it neatly behind us. I wait to one side, taking in our two cars parked together but separately. The car park is empty, except for us.

'Is everything ok?' I ask him. 'Between you and the boys.'

'Yes, of course. Why would you ask that?'

'Oh, you know...'

'Without you there to act as intermediary, you mean?'

'Well, yes, I suppose.'

'It's actually better.'

'Better?'

'Yes, Kate, better. It feels... Well, it just feels easier without you there, more relaxed somehow.'

'Oh.'

I don't know what to say. I don't think he is being deliberately hurtful, but it isn't what I expected to hear.

'Don't take it the wrong way. It's not your fault. It's just, you know, when you were there, I always knew they loved you better, and you loved them better, and I didn't even mind it that much – not really. But, I suppose, well, it got in the way a bit, didn't it? I mean, you were always there between us, weren't you? Between me and them? And, now you're not, it's just easier, that's all.'

I nod. He is right, of course, but then, if he had tried harder, maybe there wouldn't have been such a gap to fill. There is no need to hold onto it though. He will have to take his place in it now, maybe has already taken it even, and I can afford to be generous. We are not such bad people. This is the start of it, I think, the beginning of the rest of our lives. The real beginning. The end, but not the end. Together, but separate. Still stretching inexorably away from one another into the distance, but in the best way possible, in the best way we can. The air has opened up between us, and around us, now. It is not so much a weight lifting as a space emptying, and it feels something like a hopeful kind of stillness, and I realise, perhaps even for the first time, that we will all breathe the better for it.

TWENTY

By the time that he eventually does call, I have given up all hope that he will. I answer the phone absentmindedly, not quite registering who it is until he speaks.

'Kate, Lily told me.'

His voice, his words, everything, smashes into me. I thought I was getting better, getting over it, but I'm not over any of it I realise. I am not over him, let alone her.

'Can we talk?'

'Of course.'

I owe him that much, at least, if nothing else.

We meet in town at a coffee shop he has suggested. I think about all the times we met in hotel rooms to avoid being seen and it all seems so pointless now that he wants to meet in such a public space anyway. Perhaps he is worried I will get the wrong idea if he suggests a hotel, that it might give me false hope, or even possibly he is thinking somewhere like this will force us both to keep something in reserve, I don't know.

He is already sitting at a table, waiting, when I get there. He stands up and waves as I walk in, but he is always the first person I notice in any room, and all gazes lead to him anyway. Even after everything that has happened, I'm still not quite prepared for how seeing him again makes me feel, that jitteriness that would usually only come from downing far too much caffeine.

I sit down opposite him and, straightaway, he takes my hands in his.

'Why didn't you tell me, Kate?'

I am not prepared for this. I am prepared for him to be angry with me still, or distant most likely, but not to be kind. I am always disarmed by kindness. Tears prick my eyes. I will not cry here, not in front of all these people, not in front of him.

I pull my hands away.

'You were ghosting me, remember?'

'Did you try to tell me then?'

I shake my head.

'No. I didn't know until it was too late.'

'But you came to the hospital?'

'Yes.'

'For me. You came to the hospital for me?'

I shrug.

'I was worried about you.'

'Lily didn't tell me then, you know. She only told me the day I rang you. I would have called sooner, if I'd known. You know that, right?'

I nod, not trusting myself to speak. I know it now, I suppose.

'Please, will you just tell me what happened?'

I take a deep breath. I owe him this, I know, it is what I have come for. It is what we have both come here for. It is not everything I have come here for.

'It was an ectopic pregnancy. There was nothing they could have done. There was nothing anyone could have done. She would have been beautiful, like you, I know she would. She had your jawline, determined, and she would have been brave like you too. Braver than me. I'm so sorry, James, I really am. I named her Aurora.'

My voice catches on the name, and I feel such a heaviness pulling down in my stomach, it is almost overwhelming. It was a name for a child who would never live, ethereal, other worldly. Not like Max or Josh, with their solid, earthy names. I realise then that I have been waiting to tell him. It's why I didn't tell Zoe before, I've kept it back for him, kept something of her only for him. I must have known I would see him again after all. And he is crying too. He pulls his sleeve down over his hand and uses it to wipe his eyes. A waitress approaches to take my order, but then thinks better of it and backs away again. Every eye is on us, on James. This time I take his hands in mine, and he grips back.

'I'm so sorry, Kate, I'm so sorry you had to go through all that alone.'

'I didn't. Zoe came. We had a service for her, just me and Zoe, but it was a proper service. And afterwards… Well, after, I took her to Antarctica. I wanted to take her somewhere there was something of both of us. She was yours too, I know that.'

He makes a kind of choking sound then, tries to clear his throat, and I would give anything not to be doing this to him, here, but I have to say it because I know it will be the only chance I get. If I don't say it now, I will never be able to.

'I know you would have wanted her,' I say. 'If she had lived. I know you would have wanted her, whatever happened. I would have got a message to you somehow.'

'Why didn't you come to Paris?'

'Why did you block me?'

'It's stupid, I see that now, after this. It all just seems so stupid. I was angry – so angry. I don't think I've ever been as angry with anyone. I wanted you to realise what you'd lost, I wanted you to come after me. I wanted a grand gesture, I suppose.'

'I did come. To Paris. After I read you were engaged. I saw you filming, outside Notre Dame.'

'You were there?'

'Yes.'

'You came all the way to Paris, but you didn't even speak to me. Why would you do that?'

'I don't know. I felt like an idiot. You were engaged. I wasn't thinking straight. You broke my heart, James, I was a mess.'

'I think it was the other way round, wasn't it?'

The waitress approaches again, in the silence, and, this time, I order a cappuccino. James orders a pot of tea. It's a lot to take in I suppose.

'I was a mess in Paris too, Kate. I couldn't work. All I could think about was you. I'd never... I'd never been in love before, I guess, never had my heart broken. Someone rang Saskia, I don't know who. She said she understood, that we should get married, that she'd put me back together again. I'd left her – not that it matters now – but I'd already left her, and she came anyway. If I'd known you were there though, that you came after all...'

'Would it have made any difference?'

I don't need to ask, because I already know the answer, and I hate myself all over again. I'd followed him all the way to Paris and yet I had still hidden myself from him, held back in the crowd, as reckless in my inaction as I have ever been.

'But it didn't work out, after all? With Saskia?'

He shakes his head, raking his hand through his hair. I look for the smile, but it doesn't come.

'It's not what people think though. It's not what you thought either, what you must have thought when you came to the hospital. It was just a really bad cocktail. She did leave me, but I didn't try and kill myself, not like everyone thinks. It just wasn't working between us, was never going to work, and she could see it too, at last, and I was relieved, that's all. Genuinely relieved it was all over, relieved that... I drank a lot that night, too much I know, but it was all the meds I was on, everything I'd been on since Paris. The studio pumped me full of so much stuff just to keep me going and then, when that didn't work, they sent me home – with Saskia. I was supposed to go back, I'm still meant to go back. Anyway, it was just a bad mix is all. And then I fell down the stairs, like a complete dick obviously, and mashed myself up and the next thing I knew I was in hospital... And it took from then until now to convince them, Mum and Dad and Lily, that is, that I was ok, that I am ok, that I don't need rehab or analysis or something. That's why she's only just told me – Lily – she was worried it would be the last straw, I suppose.'

'I'm glad you're ok now,' I say. 'Really.'

I don't know what else to add. Except, I do know what else to add and, for once, I decide to be brave. If only for this one time.

'There's something I need to say, James, to tell you. Something I would have done before, I think, if I'd been able to. I wanted to say thank you. I didn't know I could ever feel like this, the way I feel about you. It's made me feel hopeful, in a strange way, for the future. If it can happen once, it can happen again, right? And, even if it doesn't, other possibilities seem to exist for me now that didn't before. Not yet. I'm not ready yet. To let go of all this. But, one day. One day soon hopefully. And I wanted to say sorry too – properly. I wrote you a letter to say it, but your agent sent it back to me. I'm sorry I underestimated you, and I'm sorry I couldn't be the person you wanted me to be, the person you thought I was. I was just trying to control the risk. Even though I knew it was going to break me, I was trying to control the risk anyway. You were wrong in Pembrokeshire though. It wasn't that I didn't love you enough – the opposite was true. But I want you to know, I won't do that again. From now on I am determined to be brave. And I really do get it now, all my life I've played it safe, but it's taken all this just to make me see how reckless that actually was, how careless. You've shown me that. You said I'd have plenty of time to think about it, and I have. I can't change what happened then, between us, but I can promise you I will never make the same mistake again.'

And I have to say it now, this one last thing. If I don't say it now, I will never say it. So I choose risk. For once, I choose risk over regret.

'So, I have to say, I have to tell you, because, if this is going to happen, it has to be something I have made happen for myself, not something that has happened to me. I have to tell you I still love you, I think perhaps I always will. But it's more than that. I want to be with you. I want to try and find a way to be with you. Even though there are so many reasons why I shouldn't, why we shouldn't, so many things that make it impossible, I want to try anyway. And, if there is any part of you that still feels the same way and, even though I almost dare not believe it, I cannot help but hope there might be, I'm asking you if we can just do that, if we can just try. It's what I should have said when I came to Paris, I know, but I'm saying it now. I'm asking you now. Even though I know it's too late, even though I tell myself it must be hopeless, even though I know it can't be, I have to ask you anyway. And then I can walk away, and never see you again, but I will know that just for a moment I was worthy of you, of me, of us, that just for a moment I was the person I ought to have been all along. I'm not hoping you will ask me, I'm not waiting for you to ask me – I'm asking you. I'm asking you.'

He doesn't say anything. I think I must have

stunned him into something like a bewildered silence. I search his eyes to try and read them, to see into him again, like in the gallery, but I find I cannot. If I am looking for acceptance, or encouragement, or any kind of sign, it eludes me. I only see what I always expected to see. At best, uncertainty. At worst, nothingness. He feels nothing. I glance down at my untouched cappuccino.

'I'm going to go now, I think. Before I embarrass either of us anymore than I already have done.'

And, before he has a chance to answer, I am already pushing back my chair. He stands too, he still looks completely bewildered. So, I take control. I walk round to his side of the table and rest my hands on his upper arms. Reaching up, I kiss him lightly on the lips, just once, briefly. Somewhere in the coffee shop a glass is dropped to shatter on the floor, and it breaks the spell. I laugh, a genuine laugh. I realise it is the first time I have laughed properly since we ran back from that restaurant in Holborn, back in January. As I leave the shop, I see people self-consciously lowering their phones, and others not even attempting to disguise the photos they've been taking. I don't care. So what, I think, let them have their tiny little glint of extraordinary. I've had mine.

I am nearly at the tube when I hear his voice. Even amidst the traffic and the crowded lunchtime street, it is the shape of his voice that cuts through.

'Kate! Kate – wait up a minute, will you?'

I turn back and he's almost running towards me, but then he slows down when he sees that I'm waiting, and it feels like an eternity passes before he reaches me.

'I wanted to tell you something too.'

I wait.

'I would've come back to you, you know. It was why I was so relieved – after Saskia left. I had already been drinking, it's true, and I drank a lot more after that, but then I suddenly felt this over-whelming sense of relief, just pure relief, and I realised it was because I knew then that I would come and find you the next day, that I could, that I could just do that if I wanted to. It was like just one moment of absolute clarity amidst all the haze. I wasn't thinking about what I would say, or what you would say, or what we would do, all I could think about was how much I'd missed you, and how everything would feel better, how I would be better, if I could just see you again. I unblocked your number that night. That's the funny thing, if you'd rung me after that, like when I was in the hospital or after, you'd have got through anyway. And I'd have called you straightaway, but it was late, and then I'd been drinking, and, well, I didn't want you to think it was, you know, like a booty call or something...'

'I have literally never been a booty call in my life.'

'No, I know, of course not. But, anyway, the next thing I was in hospital and then all the papers were saying I'd tried to kill myself... And then it felt like I couldn't call you. I was waiting for something, I don't know what, a way to make it look better maybe, I was embarrassed I suppose, ashamed. Look, it's not because of the baby, that's all I'm trying to say, it's not because of her, or it's not only because of her. I wanted to see you anyway. I had to see you. I wouldn't have been able to stop myself, in the end. You must know that, Kate. But the thing is, I just don't share your optimism.'

'You don't?'

'No. What you said about feeling hopeful for the future, you know, with someone else. I don't feel it. I mean, what if it's only going to happen once? What if this is it for us? You are right that I still want you, and I do still want to be with you, I always have, right from the start. I've never wanted anything so much. But I love you too, you see, and, unlike you, I don't think I ever will feel this way about anyone else. In fact, I'm sure I won't. So, I'm sorry, but I don't want to try. I can't. It's not enough for me. Not now. I want to make it work. I mean, really make it work. Not like us, but not us. It has to be us, as in really us. Life, as in real-life. For real. Because, I promise you, it's not going to be easy, this thing, us, and, when it gets hard – god knows, it will – I need to know you won't just throw it all away, throw us away, because of – what exactly? I don't even know. I don't even know what your objections are. I never did.'

'I don't have any objections.'

'You don't?'

He dips his head towards me at last. If he doesn't kiss me soon, I think I will scream.

'Not any. I thought I had made that abundantly clear back there.'

'Not really, not exactly…'

He's cupping my face in his hands now, and he rests his forehead against mine for just a second. I can't wait any longer, my mouth is already searching for his. It starts now. Today. It doesn't have to be forever, we can make it work one moment at a time. It's just one day and then another one, one after the other, with a night in between, that's all it needs to be. That's all it ever needs to be.

'Kate, will you just do one thing for me please?'

I used to think I would find it hard to refuse him anything. Now I know that I can't.

'Whatever you want.'

I don't care what it is, I just don't want him to ever stop kissing me again.

'Wear that fucking ring I got you.'

ABOUT THE AUTHOR

Hollie Hughes

Hollie Hughes is best known as the author of many much-loved picture books for young children but, when not scribbling away on picture book texts, she occasionally writes stories, poems and plays for older children and grown-ups too.

For upcoming publications and events, please visit www.holliehughes.com

BOOKS BY THIS AUTHOR

Potential: Short Stories And Poems For Grown-Ups

Magic Mum And The Fantabulous Fudge Pot

The Famishing Vanishing Mahoosive Mammoth

Ninja Nan

Princess Swashbuckle

The Girl And The Dinosaur

Unicorn And Me

Goodnight, Sleep Tight

Printed in Great Britain
by Amazon